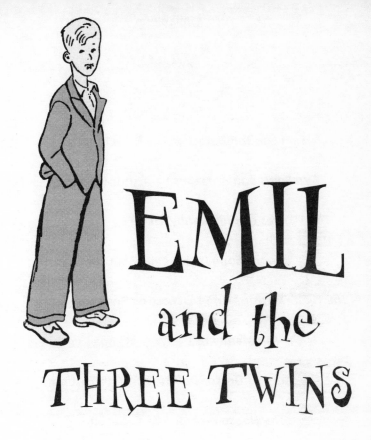

EMIL
and the
THREE TWINS

D0995924

Also available in

Red Fox Classics

EMIL and the THREE TWINS

ERICH KÄSTNER

Translated from the German by Cyrus Brooks

Illustrated by Walter Trier

RED FOX

A Red Fox Book

Published by Random House Children's Books
61-63 Uxbridge Road, London, W5 5SA

A division of The Random House Group Ltd
London Melbourne Sydney Auckland
Johannesburg and agencies throughout the world

Copyright © Erich Kastner 1935
Translation by Cyrus Brooks 1935

First published in Great Britain by Jonathan Cape in 1935
First Red Fox edition 1994
This Red Fox edition 2002

5 7 9 10 8 6 4

This book is sold subject to the condition that it shall not, by way of trade or otherwise, be
lent, resold, hired out, or otherwise circulated without the publisher's prior consent in any
form of binding or cover other than that in which it is published and without a similar
condition including this condition being imposed on the subsequent purchaser.

Printed in the UK by CPI Bookmarque, Croydon, CR0 4TD

The Random House Group Limited supports The Forest Stewardship Council (FSC), the
leading international forest certification organisation. All our titles that are printed on
Greenpeace approved FSC certified paper carry the FSC logo. Our paper procurement policy can
be found at www.rbooks.co.uk/environment

Mixed Sources
Product group from well-managed
forests and other controlled sources
www.fsc.org Cert no. TT-COC-2139
© 1996 Forest Stewardship Council
FSC

THE RANDOM HOUSE GROUP Limited Reg. No. 954009

ISBN 978 0 09 943363 7

www.randomhouse.co.uk

Contents

Illustrations

Preface for Beginners

Some children have read *Emil and the Detectives* and some have not. In the pages that follow I shall call the former the "experts" and the latter the "beginners". I have to classify them like this because I am going to write a special preface for each class of child.

"Order in all things!" said Uncle Karl, and smashed the last of the plates against the wall.

We really must have two prefaces. Otherwise it might happen that old Mr. Tomnoddy brought home this new story, and his children – i.e. the little Tomnoddies – began to bawl in their excitement, "But, Daddy, we haven't read the first book yet!" And then Mr. Tomnoddy Senior would have to pack up the volume again carefully, take it back to the bookshop and regretfully inform the bookseller that he wanted his money back because he had bought the second book first.

My dear beginners, even if you have not yet read the first book, you can read and understand the second. On this point you can safely rely on me. In all matters concerning Emil Tischbein I am one of the oldest experts on either side of the North Sea.

And, by the way, it occurs to me that it might be a good plan to explain briefly what happened in the first book. Shall I? Then here goes.

But first I must ask the experts to turn over the pages till they come to the second preface. What I am going to say now is already quite well known to them.

My dear experts, excuse me for a few

minutes. We shall meet again in the second preface. Password Emil!

The previous book told the story of what happened to Emil Tischbein, a schoolboy from Neustadt, on his first visit to Berlin.

Emil was given a hundred and forty marks to take to his grandmother in Berlin, but the money was stolen from him while he was asleep in the train.

Emil was suspicious of a man by the name of Grundeis who wore a bowler hat. But Emil was not really sure that this Herr Grundeis was the thief, and also Herr Grundeis was no longer in the railway-carriage when the boy woke up. You can imagine how terribly cut up Emil was. When the train stopped at the Zoo Station, Emil looked out of the window, caught sight of a man in a bowler hat and pursued that bowler hat, carrying his suitcase and a bunch of flowers. But really he ought not to have got out till he reached the next station, which was Friedrich Strasse.

Bless my soul! The bowler hat was actually Herr Grundeis. He got into a tram, and Emil scrambled as quickly as possible on to the trailer-car. And so the schoolboy from Neustadt, without so much as a penny in his pocket, was carried through the strange, vast city of Berlin. He was on the scent of his hundred and forty marks, and yet he was not even sure that Herr Grundeis was the thief.

Meanwhile Emil's grandmother and his cousin, Pony Hütchen, were waiting for him at Friedrich Strasse station. The train from Neustadt duly arrived, but no Emil. They did not know what to make of it. Finally they walked home, very much worried. That is to say Emil's grandmother walked – Pony Hütchen rode along on her little bicycle at her pedestrian grandmother's side.

Herr Grundeis alighted from the tram at the corner of Kaiser Avenue and Trautenau Street and sat down at a table on the terrace of the Café Josty. (Of course he had not the ghost of an idea that he was being followed.)

Emil too got off the tram and hid behind a newspaper kiosk. A boy came up to him and Emil told him just what had happened. This boy was called Gustav with the Hooter, because he carried a hooter in his trouser-pocket.

Then Gustav dashed through the neighbouring streets, loudly sounding his hooter and alarming his friends. He brought them back to Emil and they held a council of war. They pooled all their pocket money and organized a reserve detachment, a private telephone exchange and other essential services.

And when the unsuspecting Herr Grundeis had finished his meal on the café terrace and driven off in a taxicab, Emil and the detectives drove after him in a second taxi.

Herr Grundeis took a room in the Hotel Kreid at Nollendorf Square, so Emil and his

friends made their headquarters in the court-
yard of the theatre opposite. Gustav however
followed up the man in the bowler hat and
became for one night the lift-boy in the Hotel
Kreid. Thus the detectives learned that Herr
Grundeis intended to get up at eight o'clock
on the following morning.

Well, the next morning, when Herr Grundeis went to the window, the whole of
Nollendorf Square was crowded with
children!

But I must not tell you too much. Any real
boy can imagine for himself how the pursuit
went on. I want to add only that Herr Grundeis was really the thief, and his name was not
merely Grundeis but at least half a dozen
other things as well. That is generally so with
really high-class criminals.

Yes, and if Emil had not had a safety-pin in
his pocket when he was in the train, Detective
Inspector Lurje would probably have been
unable to return the hundred and forty marks

to him. The safety-pin was the final proof. But that is all I am going to tell you now. I am not going to say a single word, for instance, about the thousand-mark reward. Nor about the statue of the Grand Duke Karl, with his face all skew-whiff, nor the red nose and moustache that somebody gave him one day. Nor about Sergeant Jeschke who came after Emil with a railway-train drawn by twelve horses. And I am going to keep to myself the fact that Emil's mother came to Berlin.

You must be able to hold your tongue when necessary.

All I am going to add is that, when it was all over, Emil's grandmother said, "Money should always be sent by money order." She was, as you see, a very wise old woman. But not only *was* she, she still is. You will meet her presently. But first I must get the preface for the experts printed.

Of course, those experts!

Preface for experts

Two years after Emil's adventures with Herr Grundeis I had a very strange experience at the corner (you will remember it) of Kaiser Avenue and Trautenau Street.

I was going to take a 177 tram to Steglitz. Not that I had anything special to do in Steglitz, but I like wandering about parts of the city that are strange to me and where I am a stranger. I can pretend that I am in some foreign country. And when I feel thoroughly lonely and fed up, I make for home as fast as I can and sit snugly in my flat drinking hot coffee.

That is the sort of man I am, you see.

But I was never to take that cruise to Steglitz.

For as the tram came up with a grinding of brakes and as I was on the point of getting in, a very remarkable man got out. He was wearing a black bowler hat and he looked round as though he had a rather shop-soiled conscience. He hurried away from the tram, crossed the street, and went into the Café Josty.

I looked after him in deep thought.

"D'you want to get on?" asked the conductor.

"If you've no objection," I said.

"Then hurry up," said the conductor sharply.

But instead of hurrying up I stood rooted to the spot and stared dumbfounded at the trailer.

For there a boy was just getting out. He was carrying a suitcase and a bunch of flowers wrapped in tissue-paper, and he stopped and looked round. Then he lugged his case to a spot behind the newspaper kiosk on the corner, put it down and took stock of his surroundings.

The conductor was still waiting for me to get on. "Well, I've waited long enough," he said suddenly. "If you don't want to come, you can do the other thing!" He pulled the cord and the 177 tram set off for Steglitz, leaving me behind.

The man in the bowler hat had sat down at a table on the café-terrace and was speaking to the waiter. The boy peeped out furtively from behind the kiosk and kept his eyes on the man.

I was still standing there looking like a ninny. (By the way, do you know how ninnies look? I don't.)

It simply took my breath away! Two years ago Herr Grundeis and Emil Tischbein had alighted from the tram at exactly the same spot. And now the whole thing seemed to be

happening over again. There must be something wrong somewhere, I thought.

I rubbed my eyes and looked again at the
Café Josty. But the man in the bowler hat
was still there. And the boy behind the kiosk
sat down wearily on his suitcase and
appeared very dejected.

I thought to myself: "The best thing I can
do is to go over and ask him what's the meaning of it all. And if he tells me someone has
robbed him of a hundred and forty marks,
I'll climb the nearest tree."

So I went to the boy sitting there on the
case. "Good afternoon," I said. "Is anything
the matter?"

He made no reply, but went on staring
hard at the café.

"You haven't been robbed of a hundred
and forty marks, have you?" I inquired.

He looked up and nodded. "Yes," he said.
"It was him – that beast over there on the
terrace."

I was about to shake my head in despair and climb the nearest tree, as I had promised, when I heard a loud hooting. We both jumped and looked round. But there was no car behind us, only a boy, who was laughing at us.

"What do you want here?" I asked.

He hooted again. "My name's Gustav," he said.

My mouth dropped open. It all seemed sheer lunacy. I wondered if I wasn't dreaming.

Then a strange man came running across Trautenau Street, waving his arms. He stopped in front of me. "Get to blazes out of here!" he shouted. "Can't you mind your own business? You're spoiling the whole shot."

"What sort of a shot?" I asked curiously.

"You must have a pretty low type of intellect!" answered the man rudely.

"It's a congenital defect," I explained.

PREFACE FOR EXPERTS

The two boys laughed. And Gustav with the Hooter said to me, "Can't you see we're shooting a film here?"

"Of course," said the boy on the suitcase. "The Emil-film. And I'm playing Emil."

"You'd better be getting along," said the film-man. "Celluloid's expensive stuff."

"I apologize for the slight interruption," I said. Then I went on my way. The man ran to a big motor-car on which was mounted a film-camera. A cameraman, standing on the car, began turning a handle.

I sauntered thoughtfully to Nicholas Square and took a seat on one of the benches. I sat there for a long time, looking straight in front of me, slightly bewildered. I had known that the story of *Emil and the Detectives* was to be filmed, but I had forgotten it. Well, if you run up against a story like this for the second time after two years, with suitcases, bunches of flowers, hoots and bowler hats, it is really no wonder if your eyes stick out of your head with astonishment . . .

Suddenly a very tall, spare man sat down at my side. He was older than I, wore pince-nez, and looked at me with a smile. After smiling a bit, he said: "A funny business, eh? You think you are experiencing something real, and all the time it's only an imitation." Then I think he said that art was only an illusion of reality. But he was not trying to make himself offensive, so for a while we went on talking like that. When we could not think of any more to say about it, he added, "This peaceful seat will soon be used for the detectives' council of war."

"How do you know that?" I asked. "Have you anything to do with the film?"

He laughed. "No, no. I'm waiting here for my son. He's going to give an expert opinion on it. He was one of the real detectives."

I pricked up my ears and looked at my

neighbour more closely. "May I attempt to guess who you are?"

"You may," he said, smiling.

"You are Herr Haberland, the Professor's father."

"Quite right!" he said. "But how did you know? Have you read *Emil and the Detectives*?"

I shook my head. "No. I wrote it."

That pleased Herr Haberland enormously. And in a few minutes we were talking away like old school friends. Suddenly we became aware of a schoolboy, standing by the bench with his cap in his hand.

"Oh, here you are, old man," said Herr Haberland.

I recognized the Professor immediately. He had grown – not a lot, but still quite noticeably. I held out my hand.

"Why, it's Herr Kästner," he said.

"It is," I answered. "And how do you like the film they are making of your story?"

The Professor settled his glasses more comfortably on his nose. "They're doing their best, I admit, but a film like this ought to be written and photographed by boys. It's not a job for grown-ups."

His father laughed again. "He's still called the Professor, but he ought to have been promoted long ago."

Then the Professor sat down between us and told me all about his friends. He told me of Gustav with the Hooter, who now had a motor-cycle to go with it, and Little Tuesday, whose parents had gone to live at Dahlem – though he often came up to town, for he did not like to be so far away from his old friends – and Mittler and Gerold and Kaus and Brunner and Meyer. He told me a lot of news. The bad boy Peters had not changed much from two years before: he was still the same nasty, sneaky sort of chap, and they were always having trouble with him. "But what do you say to this?" asked the Professor.

"I've just become a householder." He sat up straight and looked terribly proud of himself.

"I'm nearly three times your age," said I, "and I'm not a householder yet. How on earth did you do it?"

"He inherited the house," explained his father, "from a great-aunt who died a short time ago."

"It's by the Baltic Sea," went on the Professor cheerfully. "And next summer I'm going to invite Emil and the detectives to stay with me." He hesitated. "That is, if Dad and Mother will let me."

Herr Haberland looked at his son through the corner of his eye. And they both looked very funny, peering at the other through their spectacles. "If I know your parents," said Herr Haberland, "they won't dare to object. The house belongs to you. I'm only its guardian."

"Then that's settled," said the Professor. "And if I get married some day and have children I shall treat them just exactly as you treat me."

"Assuming you get such a model son as mine," said Herr Haberland.

The boy leaned close to his father. "Thanks, Dad."

And that was the end of our talk. We got up, all three, and walked round to Kaiser Avenue. The actor who was playing the part of Herr Grundeis was standing on the terrace of the Café Josty. He had taken off his bowler hat and was mopping his brow with his handkerchief. In front of him were standing the director, the camera man and the chap who had ticked me off by the kiosk.

"I won't stand it any longer!" declared angrily the actor who was playing Herr Grundeis. "It's enough to ruin my digestion. I have to eat two eggs! It's in the shooting-script. Two and no more! Now I've eaten eight eggs already and still you say the shot's no good."

"What's the use of talking like that?" cried

the director. "That shot's got to be done again, old man."

The actor put on his bowler hat, looked at the sky with a pained expression and beckoned the waiter. "Two more eggs!" he said miserably.

The waiter jotted down the order and shook his head. "That film's going to cost an awful lot," he muttered, and hurried away.

Firstly: Emil himself

Here he is again. More than two years have passed since we last saw him, and meanwhile he has grown. He also has a new blue-serge Sunday suit, with long trousers of course. But if the boy goes on growing at this rate he will be able to wear them next year as shorts. He has not changed much otherwise. He is still content

to be the same excellent young fellow. He is just as fond of his mother as ever he was. And when they are together sometimes he says impatiently, "I hope I shall soon earn a lot of money, and then you'll be able to give up working." And she laughs and says, "Splendid! I shall be able to spend my time catching flies."

Secondly: Police Inspector Jeschke

The caption is quite correct. Sergeant Jeschke of Neustadt is now an Inspector. That affair of painting the statue has long been forgotten. And when he is off duty the Inspector sometimes calls on the Tischbeins and has a cup of coffee. He always buys a large slab of cake at Wirth's, the baker's, and takes it with him. Frau Wirth is a customer of Frau Tischbein's, and she said recently to her husband, the baker, "Haven't you noticed anything, Oscar?" And added, when he shook his head, "Some people are as blind as bats."

Thirdly:
The Professor's
Legacy

THIRDLY: THE PROFESSOR'S LEGACY

So this is the house that was left to the Professor by his great-aunt. It is situated at Korlsbüttel on the Baltic Sea. Somewhere between Travemünde and Zinnowitz. While she was alive, the Professor's deceased great-aunt was passionately fond of gardening. So the garden which surrounds that old one-storeyed house is well worth seeing. The shore is quite near; you can run down in your bathing-suit. Three minutes through a dusky-green coppice of alders and you find yourself on the dunes with the Baltic spread out below you. The wooden landing-stage, where the coastal steamers put in, reaches almost to the horizon.

Fourthly:
Gustav with the
Hooter

FOURTHLY: GUSTAV'S HOOTER

Have you heard the story of the man who found a button and had a suit made to fit it? The same sort of thing happened to Gustav. At first he had only a hooter. Then he kept on worrying his father till he gave him a motor-bike. Of course it is not a very big motor-bike, but the kind one can ride in Germany without a licence. But Gustav makes quite enough noise with it to please the neighbours. When he starts it up or comes careering round the corner, you would think that at least the champion motor-cyclist of Germany was coming. Meanwhile his home-work is somewhat neglected. "Well, old man," says Gustav, "I shall get through school all right somehow. I'm bottom but one, and that's good enough for me."

Fifthly:
Fräulein Hütchen

When a boy reaches the age of fourteen he
is still a boy, unless of course he is a little
beast. But when a girl reaches the same age
she becomes a young lady.
And woe to anyone who
forgets it! "Don't give
yourself such airs, kiddie!"
– You just try saying that
and you will probably have
the surprise of your young
life. Of course in the last
two years Pony Hütchen
has not become a little
prig. She is much too good
a sort for that. But she
used to be half a boy and
now she is half a flapper.
Her grandmother often

says to her, "Take your time, my dear, take your time! You'll be an old woman quite soon enough."

Sixthly:
The Railway-Steamer

SIXTHLY: THE RAILWAY-STEAMER

Have you ever seen a steam ferry-boat? They are remarkable things. They come up to the station, open their jaws and suddenly a train steams on to them. Then they set off across the water with a whole railway train in their insides. When they land, the train steams off the ship and goes on straight across country as though nothing had happened. What do you think of that? It's fun travelling by rail and it's fun travelling by steamer, but what fun it must be to travel on the railway-steamer!

Seventhly:
The Three Byrons

The Three Byrons play a quite important part in our story. They are acrobats and do their stuff in music-halls, or sometimes in circuses or cabarets. The one Byron is the father and the other two are the sons. The sons' names are Mackie and Jackie. They are twins, but Jackie is bigger than Mackie. Byron Senior is very much annoyed about it. But what is Jackie to do? He is growing. Other little boys like to grow, but Jackie Byron could kick himself for it.

Eighthly:
An Old Acquaintance

What you see here is a piccolo. A piccolo is a boy who works in a hotel and will later on become a waiter. Or head-waiter. Or reception clerk. At present he is still a piccolo and helps to lay the tables and carry the plates. Being a piccolo is a strenuous job, though one occasionally has a few hours to oneself. Then one can rush off to the beach and swim out to the sandbank. Or sit on the great rubber tube which advertises toothpaste. And then one may even meet old acquaintances from Berlin and remember times long past.

Ninthly:
Captain Schmauch

You can see a thousand yards against the wind that the above is an old sea-dog. He is the captain and owner of a tramp steamer with which he steams round the Baltic. Sometimes he has a cargo of timber, sometimes of coal, sometimes of iron from Sweden, and sometimes he is full up with rum. Oh yes, that happens now and then. The sea-wind makes him thirsty. Captain Schmauch has a cottage in Korlsbüttel and a tight little sailing boat in the harbour. And – before I forget it – the piccolo is his nephew. There are a good many more relations in the world than you would think.

Tenthly:
The Island with the
Palm

TENTHLY: ISLAND WITH THE PALM

In the midst of the Baltic Sea, not far from the coast, is a tiny little island. Some time ago a fisherman rowed over to the island with a palm in a flower pot and planted it in the sand for a joke. And now the African palm grows among the horsehair oats in that northern sand and has become quite sturdy. It would make a dog weep to see it, if there were dogs on the island, but there are no inhabitants of any sort. For one thing it consists entirely of sand and for another it is too small to live on. If you went to sleep and fell out of bed, you would find yourself in the middle of the Baltic.

And now the story can begin.

Chapter 1

INSPECTOR JESCHKE MAKES A REQUEST

Inspector Jeschke was off duty for the afternoon. He had arrived at the Tischbeins' with a packet of very noteworthy cakes, and Emil's mother had made the coffee.

Now the three of them were sitting at the round table in the parlour developing a healthy appetite. The large cake-dish gradually grew empty. Emil was getting short of breath. And Herr Jeschke was saying that the mayor of Neustadt wished to abolish the old horse-trams and lay down in their place an up-to-date electric tramway. It was only a question of money.

"Why not an underground railway while he's about it?" asked Emil. "If they get rid of our old horse-trams Neustadt won't be half so nice. There are electric trams practically everywhere."

"If it's a question of money," said his mother, "we shall keep the horse-trams till the Day of Judgment."

At that Emil heaved a sigh, took the last slice of cake from the dish and proceeded to do his duty.

The inspector politely asked permission to smoke. "Of course, Herr Jeschke," said Frau Tischbein. So her guest took a big black cigar from his leather case, lit it and wrapped himself in clouds of thick, bluish-grey smoke.

Frau Tischbein got up, collected the plates and cups and carried them into the kitchen. When she came back she said she had to run to the chemist's to get some disinfectant soap. In an hour's time Frau Homburg would be coming in for a shampoo.

Emil rose and swallowed the last mouthful of cake.

"No, no, dear," cried his mother. "I'm going myself."

The boy looked at her in surprise.

Herr Jeschke glanced over at Frau Tischbein, inhaled too much smoke and began to cough. "Emil," he said, when he had finished coughing, "I want to speak to you. As man to man."

The hall-door slammed. Frau Tischbein had gone.

"Certainly," said Emil. "Just as you like, though I don't see why Mother should go away. Running errands is really my job."

The inspector put his cigar in the ashtray, crossed his legs and flicked some ash from his coat. (Actually there was no ash there.) "I think your mother went out," he said, "so that we two could talk to each other in peace." Then he looked awkwardly at the ceiling.

Emil also looked at the ceiling, but there was nothing unusual to be seen there.

The inspector took his cigar from the ashtray, and asked suddenly: "Do you dislike me very much?"

At this Emil nearly fell off his chair. "What makes you ask that? It's a funny question, Herr Jeschke." He thought for a moment. "I used to be very frightened of you at one time."

The inspector laughed. "On account of that statue?"

The boy nodded.

"When we were boys we used to get into just such scrapes."

Emil stared at him. "What, you?"

"Absolutely," said the policeman.

"Then I like you," said Emil.

Herr Jeschke seemed pleased. "I've got something very important to ask you," he went on. "I spoke to your mother about it last Sunday. But she said it all depended on you. Without your approval nothing would come of it."

"Oh," said Emil. He reflected for a moment. "Don't be annoyed with me," he said presently, "but I don't understand a word of what you're saying."

The inspector studied his cigar. It had gone out, so he carefully lit it again. "It's hard to explain what I want to a big fellow like you," he continued. "Do you remember your father?"

"Hardly at all. I was only five when he died."

The inspector nodded. Then he said very quickly: "I want to marry your mother." He went off into a long-drawn fit of coughing. "I can get a station-job," he continued, when he had sufficiently recovered. "And later on I shall be superintendent. I'm quite sure I can pass the exam. I never went to a secondary school, of course, but I'm not altogether a fool. As superintendent I should have a very nice salary. You could even go to college if you wanted to."

Emil flicked a few crumbs of cake from the bright-coloured table-cloth.

"If you don't like the idea," said the inspector, "she won't have me."

The boy rose, went over to the window and looked out into the street. Then he turned round and said softly: "I've got to get used to the idea first, Herr Jeschke."

"Of course."

Emil looked out of the window again. "I never imagined that this could happen," he thought to himself, while his eyes followed a passing lorry. "I wanted to earn enough for her to give up working. And I wanted us two to live together all our lives. Just us two and no one else. And now a policeman comes along and wants to make her his wife!"

Just then his mother came round the

corner. She crossed the road quickly, looking straight in front of her.

Emil drew the curtain to hide his face. "Now I must decide," he thought. "And I must not think of myself. That would be mean. She's never thought of herself . . . She's evidently fond of him. I mustn't on any account let them see that I'm feeling miserable. In fact I must appear to be happy, or I shall spoil *her* happiness."

He drew a deep breath and turned round. "I agree, Herr Jeschke."

The inspector got up, crossed the room and squeezed Emil's hand.

Then the door opened. Emil's mother came quickly into the room and looked questioningly at her son.

Like lightning he remembered that he had to look happy. He laughed and put his arm through Jeschke's. "What do you think, Mummy?" he cried. "Herr Jeschke has just asked for your hand in marriage."

When Frau Homburg came for her shampoo, Inspector Jeschke, now engaged to be married, went happily away. But he came back to supper and brought a bunch of flowers, half a pound of cooked meat and a bottle of wine. "For the toasts," he said.

So after supper they drank toasts. Emil made a solemn speech, which caused Herr Jeschke to laugh heartily. Frau Tischbein sat contentedly on the sofa, stroking her son's hand.

"My dear boy," said Herr Jeschke. "Thank you for all the nice things you've said. I'm very happy indeed, and I have only one request to make: I don't ask you to call me father – that would seem a bit strange. I'm sure I shall act like a father to you, but that's a different matter, and it doesn't mean that you should call me by that name."

Emil was secretly much relieved by these remarks. "Yes, sir," he said aloud. "But how am I to address you? 'Good morning, Herr Jeschke' – that would get to sound a bit odd after a time, wouldn't it?"

The inspector rose to his feet. "First of all we two must drink to brotherhood."

So they drank to brotherhood.

"And if in future you should feel the need to call me by name," went on Herr Jeschke, "I should like to remind you that I was christened Heinrich. Have you got that?"

"Yes, Heinrich," said Emil.

And his mother laughed, so Emil felt happy.

When Heinrich Jeschke had gone home, the two Tischbeins retired. As usual they kissed each other good-night and then they went to bed. But although they pretended to be asleep, both lay awake for a long time.

Emil thought: "She didn't notice anything. She doesn't know how miserable I feel. Now she can marry Herr Jeschke and be as happy as I've always wanted her to be. He seems a nice man."

And Emil's mother thought: "I'm so glad the boy didn't notice anything. He must never find out that I would rather live with him and no one else. But I must not think of myself; I must consider my boy and his future. Who knows how long I can go on getting a living? And Herr Jeschke is such a nice man."

Chapter 2

LETTERS TO AND FROM BERLIN

When Emil came home from school next day, his mother handed him a letter. "This is for you," she said, "from Berlin."

"From Pony Hütchen?"

"No. It's in a strange handwriting."

"Then what's it about?"

"But Emil!" cried Frau Tischbein in surprise. "I wouldn't open your letters!"

He laughed. "Oh, I say, how long have we had secrets from each other?" Then he ran into the next room with his satchel, thinking to himself: "Since yesterday, since Herr Jeschke turned up!" Presently he came back, sat down on the sofa and opened the letter.

"My dear Emil,

"It's a long time since you heard from me, isn't it? All the same I hope everything is going well with you. I cannot grumble. A great-aunt of mine died a few weeks ago, but I hardly knew her, and you don't feel very sad when people like that die, do you?

"And that brings me to the real reason for writing you. My great-aunt has left me a house. It's on the Baltic Sea, at Korlsbüttel, if you've ever heard of the place. It's a seaside resort. My house also stands in a rather large and very fine garden.

"Now do you know what I'm getting at? Listen! The summer holidays will soon be here, and since I've become a householder I've had a grand idea.

"I want to invite you and the detectives to spend the summer holidays on my estate by the Baltic.

"My people have given their permission and would be very pleased. Really and truly. Of course they will be staying in the house too, but that need not make any difference to us. You know how well I get on with my dad and mother. Besides the house has an upper floor, so what more can you ask?

"Gustav has already accepted and got his parents' permission. But he's not the only one who wants to come. There are also – hold tight! – your cousin Pony Heimbold, generally called Pony Hütchen, and your grandmother whom we were all so fond of. They will come if you do, and so will Little Tuesday – provided his mother does not have to go to Nauheim. If so, he will have to go with her. It all depends on the doctor and whether he says she is fit to go to the seaside. She has something wrong with her heart.

"You see, it's going to be a grand holiday. So just pull yourself together and say Yes, you old brigand. I am sure your mother won't object when she knows your grandmother and Pony will be there. What do you think? We will meet you at the station when you arrive in Berlin, just to make sure that you do not get out at the wrong station again. And then we shall all drive to the Stettiner Station and take the train to the Baltic – to my house.

"Before I forget it – it is not going to cost you anything. We shall take our servant Klotilde with us. She is a wonderful cook, so we shall not need to spend much money. And a few more mouths to feed don't make any difference, Mother says.

"Father says I am to tell you that he is going to pay the fares. You see, my aunt left some money as well as the house, but she left the money to my dad, not to me.

"You have only to write and say you are coming, and he will send you the fare by return. I am looking forward awfully to seeing you again. I ought to apologize for talking about money. You once said that when people had money they did not talk about it. I have not forgotten that. But I cannot help speaking of it now, because otherwise you might not be able to come. And then I should not enjoy the holiday a bit. And the whole Baltic would be a washout, so to speak.

"Dear old Emil, I'm looking forward awfully to hearing from you. Kind regards from my parents and myself.

"Ever yours,

"Theodore Haberland

"(The Professor).

"Nota bene: A few months ago, shortly after I was left my house, they made the

Emil-film here in Berlin. I've seen it. It is very queer when a true story is suddenly made into a film. It is very similar, and yet quite, quite different. That is what my father thinks too. We met Herr Kästner again – the man who paid your fare on the tram and had your photograph taken for the papers. The film is to be released very soon. I'm looking forward to it, aren't you? Once more, all the best, and write soon.

"The Professor.

"Nota optime: Before I forget it – Password Emil!"

When Emil had finished reading the letter, he handed it to his mother and went into the next room. There he opened his satchel, took out his geometry book and pretended to be doing his homework. But he stared straight in front of him, thinking very hard.

"It would be a very good thing for me to go to the seaside," he thought. "I would rather stay here, of course, but I might be in Herr Jeschke's way. Not much, but perhaps a little bit. After all, since yesterday he's been engaged to Mummy. And she's fond of him. I'm her son and I've got to remember that!"

Frau Tischbein was pleased with the letter from the Professor. Her Emil would have a wonderful holiday! "Of course I shall miss him every minute of the day, but I mustn't let him know that." She went into the room where he was sitting.

"Mummy," said Emil. "I think I shall accept that invitation."

"Of course you will," she returned. "It's such a charming letter, isn't it? But you must promise me you won't swim out too far – there might be a big wave, or a whirlpool. I shouldn't have a minute's peace."

He gave his solemn promise.

"But I don't like the idea a bit of Herr Haberland paying your fare. We'll get it out of the savings bank. It won't ruin us." She stroked the boy's head as he sat over his exercise book. "Worrying your head with that homework again? Go and get a bit of fresh air before dinner."

"All right," he said. "Can I fetch anything or do any jobs for you?"

She pushed him to the door. "Out with you! I'll call you as soon as dinner's ready."

Emil went into the yard, seated himself on the steps that led down to the wash-house and thought hard while he picked the blades of grass from between the worn steps.

Suddenly he jumped up, raced through the gate and down the street, turned into Sporer Lane, ran through Weber Lane, stopped in the market-place and glanced round as though he were looking for someone.

In front of him were arrayed the canvas-covered stalls of fruiterers and greengrocers, the earthenware batteries of the potters, the stands of butchers and nurserymen. And through the variegated display sauntered

Inspector Jeschke, exercising official supervision, his hands crossed in a dignified
manner behind his back.

He stopped in front of a coster-woman.
She waved her arms. He drew his notebook
from between the buttons of his coat, entered
an important note in it, and walked gravely
on. Buyers and saleswomen put their heads
together and whispered.

Emil made his way across the uneven
cobble-stones till he came to the inspector.

"Hello!" cried Jeschke. "Are you looking
for me?"

"Yes, Herr Jeschke – that is, yes, Heinrich,"
replied Emil. "I wanted to ask you a question. A friend of mine in Berlin has had a
house left him at the seaside, and he's invited
me to spend the holidays there. My grandmother and Pony Hütchen are going too."

Herr Jeschke clapped Emil on the
shoulder. "I congratulate you. That's
splendid."

"Yes, isn't it?"

The police-officer looked down affectionately at his future stepson.

"Do you mind if I pay your fare?"

Emil shook his head vigorously. "I've got my own savings-book."

"What a pity!"

"No, Heinrich. I've come about something quite different."

"Out with it!"

"It's about Mother. If you hadn't – I mean if it weren't for you I shouldn't think of leaving her. And I shall only go if you promise me faithfully that you'll spend at least an hour with her every day. Otherwise she'll – I know just how she is and I don't want her to feel lonely while I'm away." Emil paused. Life was sometimes very difficult. "You must give me your word of honour that you'll look after her. Or I shan't go."

"I promise. And I'll give you my word of honour if you want it, old man."

"Then that's all right," said Emil. "You'll look in every day, won't you? Of course I shall write to her very often, but letters are not much, are they? There must be somebody there who's fond of her. I can't have her feeling miserable."

"I'll look in every day," promised Herr Jeschke. "For an hour at least and longer if I can manage it."

"Thank you," said Emil. Then he turned round and raced back the way he had come.

When he reached the yard he sat down on the steps again and picked the grass-blades from between the steps, as though he had never left the place.

Five minutes later Frau Tischbein looked out of the kitchen window. "Now, young man," she cried. "Come to dinner!"

He looked up with a smile. "I'm coming, Mummy."

She withdrew her head.

He got up slowly and went into the house.

That afternoon he asked his mother for some notepaper, sat down at the table, and wrote the following letter to Theodore Haberland:

"My dear Professor,

"Thank you very much for your letter, which I liked enormously. Fancy your being a house-owner! And a house by the seaside too! Congratulations! I've never been to the Baltic. But we were doing Mecklenburg and the Baltic coast in geography not long ago, and I can just imagine it all. The dunes, the big ships, the brick churches, the harbours, the chairs on the beach and so on. I think it must be marvellous.

"And it is still more marvellous of you to invite me to stay with you. I accept your invitation and thank you and your people very, very much indeed. I'm so looking forward to seeing you and Gustav and

Little Tuesday. For I'm very fond of you fellows who helped me two years ago. And I think it's just great of you to have asked Pony and Granny.

"If there isn't enough room in your house, we can pitch a tent in your garden and live like the Beduins in the desert. We can use the sheets as burnouses. And we must take it in turns to keep watch for an hour every night, so that the others can sleep in peace. But there's plenty of time to arrange that.

"I shall write to Granny and Pony to-day. It's awfully nice of you to meet me at the station. You can be sure I shan't let myself be robbed this time, even if I have to hide my money in my shoe.

"Tell your father I'm very grateful to him for his offer to pay the fare. But I'd rather take it out of my account in the savings-bank. I've still got 700 marks from that reward, you know. With the other 300 I bought my mother an electric hair-drier, as I had promised, and a warm winter coat. It still looks very nice, but my mother takes great care of her things.

"Mother says will you ask your mother whether I am to bring any bedclothes, and whether I shall need a bathing-costume. I've only got a pair of red slips, and sometimes they are forbidden at the swell resorts.

"Yes, and do you travel third class? If not we shouldn't be able to go in the same compartment. Second class is much dearer. And if you go third you get there just as soon, don't you?

"When we're in your house you must tell me all about what it was like when you watched them making the Emil-film. I hope we can soon see it in the cinema. Perhaps all together.

"Kindest regards from Mother and me to you and your parents, and once more thank you very much.

EMIL AND THE THREE TWINS

"I think it's wonderful. Password Emil!
"Ever yours,
"Emil Tischbein."

Chapter 3

EMIL MAKES A MOVE

The days and hours we dread approach with the speed of the wind; they hasten towards us like dark, heavy rainclouds, driven by the wind across the sky.

But happy days take their time, as though the year were a maze and they could not find their way out of it, least of all to us.

But the time comes when the summer holidays are here at last. You wake up at the usual early hour, and you are about to jump out of bed when you remember that there is no school today; you turn your face idly to the wall and close your eyes again.

Holidays! The word sounds like two large ices with Devonshire cream. And summer holidays too!

You look doubtfully over at the window and find that the sun is shining. The sky is blue. Not a leaf is stirring on the almond-tree outside the window. It looks as though it were standing on tip-toe and peeping into your room. You are so happy and contented that if you weren't too lazy you would do a tap dance on the wardrobe.

Suddenly you jump out of bed as though a wasp had stung you. Good heavens, you're going away! You haven't finished packing! And the clock has stopped again!

Without stopping for your slippers, you rush out of the bedroom and shout from the landing: "Mummy, what time is it?"

At last Emil was standing on the platform.

His mother was holding his hand, and Herr Jeschke, who had specially arranged to be off duty for an hour, was carrying the suitcase and the packet of sandwiches. He had retired into the background so as not to disturb them.

"And write me every other day," begged Frau Tischbein. "You promised you wouldn't swim out too far. But I shall worry about you all the same. No one can tell what will happen when all you boys get together."

"Oh come, Mummy," cried Emil. "You know me. If I give you my word, I shall keep it. But I shall be worrying about *you*, and that's worse. How on earth will you pass the time without me?"

"I've got plenty of work to do. And when I've finished, I shall go out for a walk. On Sundays I shall go into the country with Herr Jeschke, to the woods or on the river. That is, if he's free, of course, and we shall take some sandwiches with us. And if he's not free I shall do some darning. Two of my counterpanes are in a shocking state. Or I could write you a long letter. Shall I?"

"As often as you can," said Emil, and squeezed her hand. "And if anything goes wrong, send me a telegram, and I shall come straight back."

"What is there to go wrong?" asked Frau Tischbein.

"You never can tell. If you need me, I shall come. And if there doesn't happen to be a train I shall walk. I'm not a small boy any more. So don't forget it. I don't like you hiding all your troubles from me."

Frau Tischbein looked at Emil in dismay. "What do I hide from you?"

Both were silent, looking at the shining rails.

"I don't mean anything special," answered the boy. "Tonight, when we get to the Baltic, I shall write you a card. But you may not get it till the day after tomorrow. I don't know how often they clear the letterboxes at the seaside."

"And I shall write to you as soon as I get home," declared his mother. "So you'll soon have a sign of life from me. You'd feel so queer if you didn't."

Then the Berlin train came clattering in. It stopped with a deep sigh, and Herr Jeschke made a dash for a third class compartment. He reserved a seat by the window, carefully stowed Emil's case on the luggage-rack, and waited till the boy came scrambling into the carriage.

"Thanks awfully," said Emil. "You're awfully kind to me."

"Not worth mentioning, old man," said Jeschke. Then he took his purse out of his pocket, produced two five-mark pieces and handed them to Emil. "Bit of pocket-money," he explained. "It always comes in handy. Have a good time. They say the weather's going to be fine for the next few weeks.

Anyhow, it said so in the paper. You know what I promised you down in the market – I shall keep my word. Trust me! I'll drop in and see your mother every day – even if it's only for an hour."

Emil carefully pocketed the two five-mark pieces. Then he shook the inspector by the hand. "Thanks very much, Heinrich."

"That's all right, old man." Jeschke tried to push the suitcase still further back on the rack. "I don't want it to fall on your head when the train goes round a curve. And now I must clear out." He descended on to the platform and retired behind Frau Tischbein.

She came close up to the window and enjoined Emil to give her best wishes to his grandmother, Pony and all the others. "And don't go into the water when you're hot, or you might get heart failure."

"And that wouldn't be good for you!" cried Jeschke, and laughed nervously.

"Don't forget to eat your sandwiches," cried his mother, "or they'll get stale."

The station-master gave the signal to start and the train jerked forward.

"Go on loving me," said the boy. But he said it so softly that his mother did not hear it. He was glad of that afterwards.

The train drew slowly out of the station.

"And don't go disfiguring any statues!" cried Herr Jeschke, and laughed.

Then they could only wave their handker-chiefs.

This time there were neither dreams nor robberies to mar the journey.

Emil had brought with him his geography book – *Part I, Germany* – and carefully read up again the Bay of Lübeck, Mecklenburg, Pomerania, the Island of Rügen, and the Baltic Coast. It was almost like preparing for an exam.

The boy was habitually conscientious. (There are worse habits.)

When he had read these sections through twice, he shut the book and looked out of the window at the peaceful landscape through which the train was passing. As he contemplated the ripening cornfields the things he had been reading began to go round and round in his head like a dozen mill-wheels: the siege of Stralsund, the birthplace of Field-Marshal Blücher, the chalk-cliffs of Rügen, Mecklenburg cattle, charcoal-burning, juniper schnaps, Lübeck marzipan, and the landing of Gustavus Adolphus of Sweden, all merging into each other as in a rapidly turning kaleidoscope.

Emil ate his sandwiches to steady himself, finished every crumb, and threw the paper out of the window. The wind whirled it up and finally dropped it in a bed of vegetable marrows beside a signal-box. The barrier at the level-crossing was closed and a wagon was waiting in the road. A boy sitting next to the carter waved his hand. Emil waved back.

Sometimes people got out and sometimes they got in. Sometimes the guard entered the compartment and made illegible pencil marks on the backs of the tickets. So there was no lack of variety.

The train approached the capital of Germany much, much faster than on that occasion two years before.

It is always the same. Whether you are walking or going by train, the way always seems shorter the second time than the first. (And that is true of distances that are not to be measured in miles and yards.)

Emil's grandmother and Pony made their way through the barrier at Friedrich Strasse station. "Don't race so," cried Emil's grandmother. "I'm not an express train!" Her black bonnet had slipped down on one side.

"He'll be here in one minute," returned Pony impatiently. "We ought to have been more punctual."

Her grandmother shook her head vigorously, causing her bonnet to slip still farther to one side. "You can't be more punctual than punctual. Half an hour too early is just as unpunctual as half an hour too late."

Pony was on the point of disputing this statement. But the Professor had caught sight of her; he came hurrying up and raised his cap. "Good morning," he said and, taking the case from Pony's hand, cleared a way for them.

"Good morning, you landed proprietor," answered Pony's grandmother.

He laughed and led his guests to his parents. Herr Haberland shook hands with them and introduced them to his wife. Frau Haberland, the Professor's mother, was pretty and dainty and no taller than her son. Beside her long, lean husband she looked almost like a little girl.

Pony performed several curtsies and delivered the thanks and good wishes she had brought from her own parents to the Professor's father and mother. Her grandmother said she had never been to the seaside in her life and was on pins and needles to see what it was like.

Then they all stopped talking and waited for Emil. They had not long to wait. The train swept into the station with a thunderous roar and came to a standstill. The passengers began to swarm out.

"I'm sure he's got out at the Zoo again," complained Pony. But there was Emil scrambling down from his compartment, dragging his case after him and looking round for his friends. He caught sight of them, smiled, and came running forward. When he had put down his case, he gave his grandmother a kiss and shook hands with the Professor's parents. "Good heavens!" he cried to Pony. "How you've grown!"

Finally he went up to the Professor. The two boys were quite formal with each other.

But boys are always like that when they have not met for a long time. (It never lasts more than about ten minutes.)

"Gustav went off this morning on his motor-bike," exclaimed the Professor.

"Oh?" said Emil.

"I was to remember him to you."

"Thanks."

"And Little Tuesday went yesterday."

"Not to Nauheim?"

"No. The doctor said his mother was well enough to go to the seaside."

"Great!" declared Emil.

"Just what I think," agreed the Professor.

Then there was an awkward pause. But Herr Haberland saved the situation by tapping three times on the ground with his walking-stick. "Everyone listen to me! We are now going to the Stettiner Station. I'm paying for two taxi-cabs. The grown-ups will go in one and the children in the other."

"And what about me?" asked Pony Hütchen.

They all laughed. Except, of course, Pony. She was a little upset. "I'm not a child any more, and I'm not a grown-up, I suppose. What am I then?"

"A silly girl," said her grandmother. "You'll go with the grown-ups as a punishment, and that will teach you that you're still a child."

And that was all the satisfaction Pony got.

They had lunch in the waiting-room at Stettiner Station. Then they got into the train that was to carry them to the Baltic, and, having arrived early, they had a compartment to themselves in spite of the holiday crowds. The train was packed to the doors with children, buckets, flags, balls, spades, orange-peel, folded deckchairs, bags of cherries, balloons, shouts and laughter, as it steamed merrily through the pinewoods of the

Mark Brandenburg. It was a very jolly train. The noise poured out of the open windows and floated across the peaceful landscape.

As the pines swayed gently in the summer breeze, they whispered to each other: "The holidays have begun."

"I thought as much," growled an ancient beech.

Chapter Four

SEASIDE VILLA

Korlsbüttel is not one of those big seaside resorts. Ten years ago Korlsbüttel had not even a station. In those days one alighted from the Lübeck-Stralsund train at a little place which, if I remember rightly, is called Stubbenhagen. If you were particularly lucky, you found there an old-fashioned vehicle to which was harnessed a heavy Mecklenburg horse, and in this you jogged over uneven sandy lanes to Korlsbüttel. Left and right lay the heath. The juniper-bushes stood like green dwarfs between century-old oaks and beeches. And sometimes a herd of deer would flit through the silence, while pungent smoke rose into the summer air from the charcoal piles in the clearings. It was a countryside from *Grimm's Fairy Tales*.

All that has now changed. You go in a through-train to Korlsbüttel, stride nobly down the platform and hand your case to a porter. In three minutes you are in your hotel and in ten on the shore. I think it was nicer in the old days. You had to overcome obstacles then before you could get to the sea, and it is a mistake to under-estimate obstacles. They have their own uses.

Half Korlsbüttel was at the station to meet the holiday-train. The yard was full of brakes, cabs, three-wheelers, hand-carts and trucks. Many visitors were expected and a great deal of luggage.

Fräulein Klotilde Seelenbinder, the Haberlands' elderly maid-servant, was leaning against the barrier. When she saw Herr Haberland she waved both her hands. He towered a good head above the passengers who were streaming out of the train. "Here I am!" she shouted. "Herr Haberland! Herr Haberland!"

"Don't make so much noise, Klotilde," he said, and shook hands with her. "It's a long time since I saw you, isn't it?"

She laughed. "Oh, it's only two days, sir."

"Is everything all right?"

"You may be sure it is. Good evening, madam. I hope you're well. It's a good thing I came on first. A house like that makes a lot of work. Hello, Theo! You look pale, darling. Is anything the matter? And that must be your friend, Emil, isn't it? How do you do, Emil? I've heard a lot about you. The beds are all made up. There's beefsteak and mixed vegetables for supper. The meat's cheaper here than in Berlin. Oh, and there's Pony Hütchen, Emil's cousin. You can't mistake her. They're the very spit of each other. Haven't you brought your bicycle with you?"

Emil's grandmother covered her ears with her hands. "Do give us a rest!" she begged. "Give us a bit of peace, Fräulein. If you go on talking we shall have pleats in the lobes of our ears. I'm Emil's grandmother. Good evening, my dear."

"The very spit of each other!" repeated the Haberlands' maid. Then she bowed. "Klotilde Seelenbinder," she announced.

"Is that a new profession?" asked Emil's grandmother.

"No, it's my name."

"Poor thing! Why don't you go to the doctor. He might prescribe another name for you."

"Are you serious?" asked Klotilde.

"No," returned Emil's granny. "No, my dear. I'm hardly ever serious. It's seldom worth it."

Then the bags and cases were loaded on to a hand-cart, which Klotilde had borrowed from the carrier. The carrier's man pulled in front and Emil and the Professor pushed behind. Thus they went down Blücher Street. The grown-ups and Pony walked behind.

Suddenly there was a succession of loud hoots. A motor-cycle came sweeping at breakneck speed out of a side street. There was a screeching of brakes. The carrier's man brought the hand-cart to a standstill and swore till the window-panes rattled all round them. Luckily he swore in Low German.

"Don't get excited, old thing!" cried the motor-cyclist. "It's not all that important."

Emil and the Professor looked round the pile of luggage in astonishment. "Gustav!" they yelled and ran round the carrier's hand-cart to clap their old friend on the back.

The bewildered Gustav laid his motor-bike flat in the road and pushed up his goggles. "Well, if that isn't the limit!" he cried. "I jolly near made mincemeat of my two best friends!

We were just coming to fetch you from the station."

"But what can you do against fate?" asked a voice from the roadside-ditch. Gustav jumped and looked down at his motor-cycle. "What's become of Little Tuesday?" he cried. "He was on my pillion a minute ago."

They peered into the ditch. There was Little Tuesday, none the worse. He had been thrown into the air and landed in the grass at the bottom of the ditch. He laughed. "We've made a good beginning," he said. Then he jumped to his feet. "Password Emil!"

"Password Emil!" shouted all four, and went happily on their way.

The grown-ups followed at a distance. They did not even know that anything had happened.

"That's Theo's house," said Klotilde See-lenbinder proudly, as she pointed to it.

It was a charming old-fashioned building

surrounded by a garden full of trees and flowers. The name "Seaside Villa" was painted across the gable.

"To the left you'll see a big glass veranda with sliding windows," went on Klotilde. "Above that is an open balcony for sun-bathing. The room next to it I've got ready for Herr and Frau Haberland. I hope that's all right, madam?"

"Whatever you do will be all right," said the Professor's mother kindly.

The maid-servant blushed. "Then the next room is for Emil's grandmother and Pony Hütchen. We shall fix up the boys on the ground floor, in the room behind the veranda. The room next to that has a sofa in case somebody drops in and wants to stay the night. And there's a camp-bed we can put up too. You'll take your meals on the veranda, unless of course, the weather's fine enough to have them in the garden, though the food gets cold so quickly out of doors.

But you can always cover it up." She looked round. "What's become of the boys? They ought to have been here before us."

"I expect they've gone to bed," said Emil's grandmother. "And if you go on talking like this they will have had their night's sleep and be up again."

Klotilde looked doubtfully at the little old woman. "I never quite know with you whether you mean it or not."

"That requires a bit of practice," declared Pony. "My father says Granny's as slippery as an eel." Then she opened the garden gate and ran towards the house. The grown-ups followed more sedately and gave the carrier's man instructions as to what to do with the various cases and trunks.

Most of the garden lay behind the house. The four boys were exploring it in search of a garage for Gustav's motor-cycle. The Professor sat down on a bench and swung his legs. "There are two alternatives," he announced. "We must put it either in the greenhouse with the tomatoes or in the toolshed."

"It's too warm in the greenhouse," suggested Tuesday.

Emil reflected. "There's sure to be knives and other sharp instruments lying about in the toolshed. The tyres might get damaged."

Gustav ran across to the shed, looked in and shrugged his shoulders. "There isn't even room for a roller, let alone my powerful motor-bike."

The Professor laughed. "Did you say *powerful?*"

Gustav was hurt. "It's the most powerful sort you can get without a driving licence. It's quite powerful enough for me. And if I hadn't jammed the brakes on you'd all be bone-meal."

"Let's turn off the heating in the greenhouse," suggested Tuesday.

The Professor shook his head. "Then the tomatoes would never ripen."

"Do you think the tomatoes care whether they ripen or not?" cried Gustav. "It's not all that important."

Just then Pony Hütchen appeared.

Emil waved his hand to her. "Do you know of a garage for Gustav's motor-bike?" he inquired.

She stopped and looked round. Then she pointed to the end of the garden. "What's that building down there?"

"That's the so-called pavilion," returned the Professor.

"And what is it used for?" she asked.

"No idea," he answered.

They went over to the pavilion, Gustav pushing his motor-cycle in front of him.

It was a little glass house, and contained a white-enamelled table and a green watering-can.

"Fine!" said the Professor. "This place was born to be a garage."

"What would you do without me?" asked Pony Hütchen. She opened the door. The key was in the lock. Gustav pushed his machine into the pavilion and locked the door. He took out the key and put it in his pocket.

The other boys went back to the house, for they were hungry. Pony Hütchen was about to follow.

"How do you like my motor-bike?" asked Gustav.

She turned back to the pavilion, looked in through the glass and examined Gustav's machine.

"Well?" he asked. "How do you like it?"

"Extra medium grand!" she declared, and strode off like a dowager queen.

Gustav looked after her doubtfully. Then as he turned to his motor-cycle his face lit up with pride, only to take on an injured expression as he looked after Pony again. "It's not all that important," he muttered to himself.

After supper they sat for a while on the veranda, looking at the brilliant blooms in the garden. "Well, how did it taste?" asked Klotilde at last, impatiently.

Of course they were all of one opinion. And when Emil's grandmother stated that she had not eaten a nicer bit of steak since her silver wedding, Fräulein Seelenbinder was blissful.

While, with Pony's assistance, she was clearing away, Emil wrote a card to his mother. Gustav also decided to send his parents a line announcing his safe arrival. They handed their cards to Little Tuesday, whose parents had been waiting for him for some time at the Pension "Sea View". He promised to go round by the post-box.

"Don't just go round by it," said Emil. "Drop the cards in, will you?"

Then Little Tuesday look his leave. "Don't be too late in the morning!" he said, and ran off.

Herr Haberland stood at the veranda door, looking up at the sky. "It's after sunset," he said, "but we must say good-night to the sea before we slip into our beds."

Klotilde stayed behind to wash up the dishes, but the rest of them set off through the coppice of alders. They came to the end of the coppice and began to ascend the rise that led to the dunes, from which they would catch their first glimpse of the sea.

"Those who have never seen the sea step forward," said Herr Haberland.

All stood still except Emil, Pony and their grandmother.

"You go on ahead," said Herr Haberland.

So Frau Heimbold put her arms through those of her two grandchildren and walked

They found themselves on the highest point of the dunes

on in front of the others. In a few minutes they found themselves on the highest point of the dunes. To their right was the Strand Hotel. In front lay the long expanse of sandy shore, with all its deck-chairs and flags and sandcastles.

And at the edge of the shore began the sea. Whichever way they looked, there was no end to it. It seemed to be made of liquid mercury. Far off on the horizon a ship was sailing into the falling night. A few lights were twinkling. The sky still reflected the rosy light of the sun, which had already set, and in the centre of its dome hung the sickle-moon. It looked quite pale as though it were recovering from a long illness. And the first beams of distant lighthouses flitted over the pastel-coloured heavens. From far away came the howl of a steamer's siren. The two children and their grandmother were overwhelmed. They stood there in silence, feeling as though they would never speak again in their lives.

They heard the crunch of footsteps behind them, and the Haberlands and Gustav came quietly up.

Gustav went up to Emil. "It's a marvel, isn't it?" he said.

Emil only nodded.

They stood without speaking, side by side, looking steadily at the sea.

Emil's grandmother said softly: "At last I know why I've lived to be such an old woman."

Chapter 5

AN ENCOUNTER BY THE BALTIC

Next morning, as Klotilde was about to knock on the door of the boys' room, she heard the sound of giggling. "Are you awake?" she asked, and put her ear to the door.

"Awake is not the word for it," said the Professor laughing.

"Who's speaking?" asked Gustav sharply. "Who's taking the liberty of speaking to us without having been introduced?"

"It's me," cried the maid. "Klotilde."

"Aha," said Emil, "Fräulein Selbstbinder."

"Seelenbinder," corrected Klotilde testily.

"No, no," said Gustav. "We much prefer Selbstbinder. From now on we shall call you Selbstbinder, and if that doesn't suit you we'll call you Schlips! What d'you say to that, Fräulein Klotilde Schlips?"

"A most excellent name!" declared the Professor. (He still had the habit of passing judgment on things and people.) "Klotilde, you shall henceforth be called Schlips."

"You think you can do what you like with me," complained the old servant. "But listen, you've got to come to breakfast. The others are all in the garden. And I'm not going to stop here any longer."

"Goodbye, Schlips," cried the three boys. Then they goose-stepped through the veranda-door into the back garden. There was a big round table, laid for breakfast, in the middle of the lawn. The Professor's father and mother, Pony Hütchen and her grandmother had already taken their places. Herr

Haberland was reading the paper. With considerable astonishment the others watched the arrival of the three boys. Frau Haberland tapped her husband gently on the shoulder. "What is it?" he asked, putting down his newspaper. Then he joined in the general surprise.

The Professor and Gustav were in bathing-suits, Emil in his red slips, but that was not the cause of their astonishment.

The Professor was wearing his father's panama hat and swinging a heavy walking-stick. Emil had put on Pony's summer coat and her yellow straw hat with the shiny red cherries and, as he marched across the grass, he held above his head a sunshade with a gaudily striped cover. He looked like a conceited young woman who is a little soft in the head. But Gustav was the oddest of them all. He was wearing Emil's grandmother's bonnet, and had tied the black silk ribbons so tightly under his chin that he could hardly open his mouth. He was also wearing his goggles and waving Pony's handbag daintily in one hand while carrying a heavy suitcase in the other.

They did not blink an eyelid as they sat down in dead silence in their basket-chairs. Then the Professor tapped his cup with his coffee-spoon and they suddenly cried with one voice: "Good evening, ladies and gentlemen."

"The poor fellows must have got sunstroke," said Herr Haberland. "What a shame! And the holiday's only just beginning!" Then he took up his paper again.

"We ought to fetch a doctor," suggested Pony. "I warn you, my lad – don't you get my handbag dirty!"

Gustav turned round. "Waiter!" he cried. "Do you call this a restaurant?" Then he hastily untied the bonnet-ribbons. He was almost throttled. "I shan't go to that shop for my next bonnet," he muttered. "There's not a single point where it fits!"

Klotilde came out of the house with a fresh jug of coffee.

"Oh, here you are," said the Professor. "Fräulein Klotilde Schlips again. They're always the same!"

The servant poured out coffee and placed the jug on the table. "Have I got to put up with them calling me Schlips?" she asked tearfully.

"But why Schlips?" inquired Frau Haberland.

"We can't find any meaning in Seelenbinder," explained Emil.

"So we decided to call her Selbstbinder," said the Professor. "But that wasn't good enough for her."

"So we christened her Schlips," mumbled Gustav, with his mouth full. "Some people would be glad of such a name. Our sportsmaster's called Philip Ox. When he goes to a party and someone mentions his name he just has to clear out. Everybody bursts out laughing."

"Think how pleased he'd be if he was called Schlips!" said Emil.

Klotilde Seelenbinder gave it up and went silently back to her duties.

Pony looked across at her grandmother. "What's the matter with them? Is it anything serious?"

"Lord preserve us!" cried her grandmother. "It's a very common complaint. They call it adolescence."

Herr Haberland nodded. "I know it from personal experience. I had it myself once."

After breakfast Tuesday put in an appearance and took them off with him to bathe. Herr Haberland and his wife stayed at home, but the others, including Emil's grandmother, set off for the shore. The boys decided to go barefoot. It was healthier, they said.

They stopped on the top of the dunes. This morning the sea looked quite different. It shone with a greenish-blue light. And sometimes, when the wind rose, it sparkled with a golden sheen that made you shut your eyes. Emil's grandmother put on the dark glasses which Fräulein Klotilde Seelenbinder had lent her. Below them, the shore was covered as far as the eye could see with deckchairs, sand-castles, flags, pennons and people.

Sometimes a succession of waves ran across the surface of the water, and Pony remarked: "It looks as if an invisible shop-assistant was unrolling bright silk on an endless counter."

The four boys looked at each other meaningfully and said nothing, but it was too much for Little Tuesday, who burst out laughing.

"Silly idiots!" said Pony, and walked on alone towards the shore. Emil and his grandmother smiled and followed. When they had gone some distance, Emil turned and looked round for his companions. They were all standing some little way off, making no attempt to follow.

"What are you waiting for?" Emil shouted.

Slowly they began to move forward. But after a few steps they went on strike again. Gustav was hopping on one foot, grumbling volubly.

Frau Heimbold laughed. "Your friends from Berlin are not used to going barefoot. The gravel path is too sharp for them."

Emil ran back. Gustav screwed up his face. "Jove, and they say it's healthy!" he grumbled.

"I've had enough, thanks," said the Professor. "My feet are not made of ox-hide."

"Never again!" vowed Tuesday, and ventured to take one more step. He hopped like a cat on hot bricks.

Gustav stepped off the path with the intention of walking on the grass. But what looked like grass was really sand-oats, and it scratched his legs so painfully that he let out an angry "Ahoo!" and hopped back on to the gravel.

"There's a lot of silicic acid in sand-oats," remarked Emil.

"I never thought silicic acid was so prickly," said Gustav. "You might just as well walk on razor-blades."

Emil told them a little more of the construction of vegetable cells and the nature of seashore plants in particular.

"All very well," said the Professor. "You may be a whale for botany, but I'm going to run back to my house and get my gym shoes." And he did so. Gustav and Tuesday followed his example.

Emil rejoined his grandmother. They sat down on a bench and contemplated the sea. A little white coasting-steamer had just put in to the landing-stage.

The boy looked round for Pony, but she was already far ahead.

His grandmother pushed her borrowed glasses on to her wrinkled forehead. "At last we've got a moment alone together. How are you, my boy, and how's your mother?"

"Very well, thank you, Granny."

The old woman put her head on one side. "You're not very talkative, are you? Tell me some more, young man."

He looked out to sea. "But Granny, you've heard all about things in our letters! Mummy has a lot to do, but she wouldn't enjoy life if she didn't have to work. And as for me, well, I'm still top of the form."

"Oh," said the old lady. "I see. That sounds very satisfactory." And she took hold of his shoulder and gave him a gentle shake. "Will you tell me what's the matter, you scamp? There's something wrong, there's something wrong! Emil, I know your face as well as my own handbag."

"But what should be wrong, Granny? Everything's fine. Of course it is!"

She rose to her feet. "And you have the cheek to tell your granny that tale!"

At last they all arrived together on the beach.

Emil's grandmother sat down in the sand, took off her shoes and stockings and gave her feet a sun-bath. Meanwhile she kept guard over the towels they had brought.

The boys joined hands, with Pony in the middle, and ran yelling into the sea. A fat woman, who was sitting half asleep in the shallows, swallowed a good deal of water and complained vociferously.

Emil's granny turned up her skirt and walked a few steps into the water. "Were you ever young, madam?" she asked politely.

"Of course!" was the answer.

"Well then!" said the old woman. "Well then!" And without going into further detail she returned to sit in the warm sand and look happily at the jubilant children. All she could see now was their heads, and not always them.

Gustav was the fastest swimmer and the first to reach the big diving-raft, which was anchored in deeper water and on which the swimmers could lie and rest. Pony and Emil swam at about the same speed and helped each other to "land". Tuesday and the Professor arrived a little later.

"How do you do it?" asked Tuesday, when he had joined his friends on the raft. "How do you manage to swim faster than Theo and I?"

The Professor laughed. "Don't worry about that. We're brain-workers."

"I don't see what your head's got to do with it," said Gustav, "except that you keep it too high out of the water. You must learn the crawl." He rolled off the raft, fell with a splash into the Baltic, and gave them an exhibition of the crawl-stroke.

"How much d'you charge per hour?" asked Pony.

He took a deep breath, dived and remained under water for a long time before he came up gasping. "Sixty minutes," he answered.

Then they all swam shoreward. Gustav showed them the crawl again, and they tried to imitate him. In doing so, the Professor collided with a man who was swimming slowly on his back. "Look where you're going!" cried the man. "Where were your eyes?"

"Under water," answered the Professor truthfully, and made off like a ship's screw to join his friends.

They had reached the territory of the non-swimmers, and were looking at a huge, rubber toothpaste-tube. (Which was, of course, an advertisement.) They tried to clamber on to it, but as soon as they got to the top the tube turned over and dropped them with a splash into the water. There was a great deal of noise.

The friends caught sight of some bars and other gymnastic apparatus upon the beach. A man was swinging on the horizontal bar. He did a "press-up", swung forward, performed a magnificent grand-circle, suddenly brought his legs between his arms and arrived in a sitting posture on the bar. Then he let himself fall backward, spread out both arms, released the grip of his knees on the bar as his body swung forward, shot through the air, and landed in the sand with knees smartly bent.

"My hat!" cried Gustav. "That's more than I could do."

The gymnast stepped to one side and two small boys took up their positions under the bar. They jumped up, hung quite still, began to swing and repeated side by side and in perfect time the series of difficult exercises the man had just performed. They finished, as he had done, by shooting gracefully through the air and landing in the sand with knees smartly bent. The crowd of holi-day-makers on the shore clapped their hands.

"I shall go mad!" cried Gustav. "I've never seen anything like it, least of all from little kids like that."

"Those are the Three Byrons," said a boy who was standing in the water close by. "A family of variety artistes, father and twin sons. They are appearing every evening in the Strand Hotel."

"We must go and see them," said Pony Hütchen.

"The programme begins at eight o'clock," went on their informant. "The other turns are very good too. I can recommend the show most strongly."

"Is it very hard to get a seat?" asked Tuesday.

"I can reserve you a table," said the boy.

"Are you an acrobat too then?" asked Emil.

The boy shook his head. "No, I'm pretty good in the gym, but it's not my job. I'm the piccolo at the Strand Hotel."

Gustav laughed. "Piccolos die young."

"Do they?" asked Tuesday.

"Well, have you ever seen an old one?"

Pony turned up her nose. "I wish you'd stop your silly jokes."

"Gustav's grown a good deal since I last saw him," said the piccolo, "but otherwise he hasn't changed a bit."

The friends looked at each other in surprise.

"But how do you know me?" asked Gustav doubtfully.

"I know all of you," said the piccolo. "And once Gustav even wore a suit of mine."

Gustav's mouth dropped open. "What rot! I've never worn anybody else's clothes in my life."

"Oh yes, you have," said the piccolo.

The others did not know what to make of it.

"What's your name?" asked Pony.

"Hans Schmauch."

"Never heard it," said Gustav. "I don't know any Schmauchs."

"You know my father," maintained Hans Schmauch. "And so does Emil."

"This is getting more and more mysterious," Emil remarked.

Gustav waded towards the piccolo and seized hold of him. "Now out with it, young fellow, or I shall hold your head under water till you've had time to become a waiter."

Hans Schmauch laughed heartily.

"I used to be a lift-boy in Berlin. At the Hotel Kreid, Nollendorf Square. Password Emil!"

"I know all of you," said the piccolo

AN ENCOUNTER BY THE BALTIC

That put the lid on it. They danced round little Schmauch like wild Indians. The salt water splashed high into the air. Then they shook hands with him till his knuckles cracked.

"Well, this is fine!" shouted Emil. "Your father, the porter, was an absolute brick! He lent me ten marks. And Gustav and I spent the night in your room at the hotel."

"I know," said the piccolo. "That was an exciting time, wasn't it? I shall think of it all my life, even if I ever have a hotel of my own. And, I say, when I'm off duty we can all go sailing together. You see, my uncle lives here in Korlsbüttel. He's the owner of a steamship."

"But can you go sailing in a steamship?" asked Tuesday.

"Well, not quite," said the piccolo. "But my uncle's got a nice little sailing-boat too. He's a good sport."

They were pleased to hear this and ran off

up the sands to introduce Hans Schmauch to Emil's grandmother. She was as delighted as they, but not until they had all properly dried themselves.

Gustav looked at the piccolo with a grin. "There's one thing I don't understand," he said, as he rubbed himself vigorously with a towel.

"What's that?" asked Hans Schmauch, looking up at him.

Gustav shook his head. "I don't understand how I could ever have got into one of your suits."

Chapter 6

GUSTAV AND PHYSICS

There followed a succession of happy days. The sun shone as though it were watching the Baltic Sea through a burning-glass. The Professor and his guests first grew as red as lobsters and then as brown as mulattos. Only Pony Hütchen remained permanently red and began to peel like an onion. Her grandmother constantly smeared the young lady's back with vaseline, almond oil, lanoline and sunburn-lotion. But nothing did her any good.

Every morning her grandmother wakened

Pony with the words: "Get up, duchess! The sun's shining." Then Pony was on the verge of tears. "Why doesn't it rain?" she demanded in despair.

"Get into the bath, Fräulein," returned her grandmother, "and sit under the shower. Klotilde will bring your breakfast to the bathroom for a slight extra charge."

But the boys were full of enthusiasm for the fine weather. They spent most of their time in the water or on the beach. Or they went off to the harbour in the lee of the landing-stage and admired Captain Schmauch's sailing-boat *Kunigunde IV.* They looked forward to the piccolo's first day off, for he had promised to take them for a sail.

Or Gustav chugged out on his motor-cycle to the heath with one or other of his friends on the carrier. He set down his passenger at the hunting-lodge or the charcoal pile, rode back to Korlsbüttel and repeated the process until he had fetched the whole party. Once he even persuaded Emil's grandmother to let him take her to the hunting-lodge. "That was grand," she said, as she got down from the carrier. "I missed my vocation. I should have been a racing-motorist instead of a grand-mother."

Sometimes they wrote letters to their parents and sometimes they received them. Sometimes Herr Haberland took their photo-graphs and they sent home prints in their next letters.

Or they went into the woods and brought back great bunches of wild flowers. Emil was familiar with almost all the plants and told his friends their names and peculiarities. From cotton-grass to mountain ash, from sorrel to butterfly-orchids, from moss, with its mys-terious method of propagation, to cranesbill – he knew them all and told his friends about them as well as he could.

One day Herr Haberland went to Rostock and came home with a handbook of botany and an introduction to the study of plants, which he had bought at the university bookshop.

But from that day on they lost their interest in flowers, grasses and shrubs – all except Emil.

"Printed matter gives me the jitters," declared Gustav, the champion motor-cyclist.

One day Emil's grandmother received a letter from Neustadt. It was a long letter and she read it twice. Then she put it in her handbag. "Aha!" she said to herself.

But to Emil she said nothing, at least not just then.

They were enjoying their midday dinner on the veranda when Herr Haberland said: "If you have no objection, I should like to propose that we go to the Strand Hotel this evening and see the cabaret."

The boys could hardly stay to eat the

126

sweet, though it consisted of wine-jelly, and wine-jelly was one of Klotilde's specialities.

In spite of their excitement they managed to finish it, however. Then they set off like marathon-runners for the Strand Hotel. They were standing round the door, trying to decide who should go in and speak to the piccolo, when Pony Hütchen came up.

"Hello, what brings you here?" asked Gustav.

"My legs," declared Pony. "I thought I would reserve a table for this evening, if you have no objection?"

No objection was raised, so Pony went into the hotel.

The manager came up to her. "What can I do for you, miss?" he asked. "A room with a bath? Or without? Overlooking the sea? Would you like a balcony or not?"

"Not," said Pony Hütchen. "Don't exert yourself, I only want to speak to the piccolo."

The manager bit his lip. "Schmauch is in

the restaurant," he said, and, turning his back on her, retreated to the writing-room.

Pony found the restaurant. Then she found Hans Schmauch, the piccolo. He was just crossing the floor with a great pile of plates. "One moment, Pony. I won't keep you waiting."

In a moment he came hurrying back. "What is it?" he asked.

"I want to reserve a table for this evening."

"For how many persons?"

"Wait a minute, I must reckon up. There's Herr Haberland and his wife, Granny, me, Klotilde Schlips and the three boys. That's . . ."

"Eight," volunteered the piccolo. "Very good! As near the front as possible. Perhaps my uncle, the captain, will be coming. You must meet him."

"A table for nine people then," said Pony.

The piccolo bowed. "The performance begins shortly after eight."

"That doesn't matter," returned Pony. "We'll come just the same."

After supper all the occupants of "Seaside Villa" put on their best clothes and walked solemnly to the Strand Hotel. The table Hans Schmauch had reserved for them was in the front row, quite near the stage. Herr Haberland ordered wine for the adults and orangeade for the children.

It was eight o'clock but the performance had not yet begun. The orchestra played popular concert pieces one after the other, and cheery-looking holiday-makers poured into the room till presently every table was occupied.

Numerous natives of Korlsbüttel had collected outside. They peeped curiously through the windows in the hope of seeing the show for nothing. But a waiter and the piccolo crossed the room and drew the curtains. The piccolo however was less than thorough. He left wide strips of window uncovered, and winked over at the boys who were watching him.

"He's a sport," said Emil. "Now the people outside will be able to see something."

"Hans Schmauch is a humanitarian," asserted the Professor. Herr Haberland tapped Gustav on the shoulder. "How long have you been so studious? You don't generally bring books to a cabaret, do you?"

Gustav blushed. "It's an English dictionary," he explained.

"Are you going to memorize lists of words?"

Gustav shook his head. "In the holidays? What do you think?"

Pony laughed. "I know. He wants to talk to the acrobatic twins."

"That's right," said Gustav. "Their name is Byron, so they must be English. If they say anything that I don't understand, I shall simply look it up in the dictionary."

"I should like to hear that conversation," said Emil's grandmother. She was wearing a black taffeta dress and looked most impressive.

Then another guest arrived – a tall, burly man in a blue suit and a blue peaked cap. Half way across the floor he stopped and looked round inquiringly. Suddenly the piccolo hurried over to him, said a few words to him and led him to the Haberlands' table. "May I introduce my uncle, Captain Schmauch?" Then Hans was gone.

The children all stood up, and so did Herr Haberland. He shook hands with the piccolo's uncle and begged him to take a seat at their table.

The captain shook hands all round. "Don't be too formal," he said, "or I shall be off." So they all sat down again. The new arrival ordered a rum grog from the waiter. "It's fine to see such a crowd of youngsters round the table. Tell me something about your school, my lads. It's forty years since I finished my schooling. Ah, those were the days!"

The boys racked their brains, but they could think of nothing that would interest an old sea captain. He looked from one to the other. "Well, I am surprised!" he said, slapping his knee. "We must have been a very different lot when I was at school. We were up to some mischief every day!"

"Oh, that's what you want to hear, is it?" cried Gustav.

"Did you think I wanted you to say a piece of poetry?"

"The last week before the holidays," said Gustav, "I got into a scrape that very nearly finished me off. They wanted to sack me at first, but by good luck they changed their minds."

The others listened attentively.

"It was like this," went on Gustav: "during the long break before the physics lesson, the top boy of our form, a chap called Mehnert, went and blabbed to the head about one of us. Not about me, but I'm a sort of authority in my form and if anything like that happens it's up to me.

"Well, Mehnert got the wind up and kept out of sight all through break. When we were all sitting in the physics lab, he came in with old Kaul, that's the physics master. The caretaker was there too, he always helps Kaul with the experiments.

"They were going to demonstrate something about electric sparks. The length of them or something. Kaul and the caretaker set up the apparatus, and then the dark curtains were drawn across the windows so that we could see the sparks better. My neighbour, Körte, whispered to me that this was the chance of a lifetime. I was to creep round in the dark to the front row and give Mehnert a good crack across the ear. The idea was that before old Kaul could put the lights on, I should be back sitting quietly in my place.

"It seemed to me a pretty good idea. What could be better than for a sneak like Mehnert to get his medicine in public, so to speak, and yet, when the lights went up, there would be nobody to blame except, as you might say, justice in person?" Gustav looked round at his hearers. They were listening breathlessly.

"Very well," he continued. "The lab was as black as a coal-cellar. Old Kaul said the experiment was just going to begin and we were to keep our eyes open for the sparks, so while they were watching the apparatus I crept round to the front row and drew back my hand. I couldn't make a mistake for Mehnert had sat at the end of the front row for years and years.

"Well, as I say, I drew back my hand and gave him a whack that nearly cracked my wrist."

Captain Schmauch slapped his knee. "Grand! Then you sat down again and nobody knew who'd done it."

134

Gustav shook his head sadly. "No, I didn't sit down again. I had such a fright I just stood there like a dummy."

"A fright?" asked Klotilde. "What were you frightened of?"

"You see, Mehnert was bald."

"Bald!" echoed Emil.

Gustav nodded. "He had a bald head. As it happened it wasn't Mehnert at all; it was the physics master, Kaul."

Even the waiter who had brought the captain's grog was listening with both ears.

"Yes," went on Gustav. "Kaul had sat down on the bench beside Mehnert because he wanted to see the experiment for himself. That's just what you'd expect, isn't it? If a physics master isn't interested in physics, who is? But how was I to know in the dark that he'd gone and sat in Mehnert's place?"

Captain Schmauch laughed so heartily that they could not hear the orchestra, though at that moment it was playing a march.

Fräulein Klotilde Seelenbinder had turned pale. "Horrible!" she whispered. "It's made me go all goose-flesh."

Herr Haberland leaned forward. "And what happened then?"

Gustav scratched his head. "It's not all that important," he said. "But still there have been times when I've felt more comfortable. Well, somebody suddenly switched on the lights. And there was Kaul sitting in Mehnert's place, holding his bald head in both hands. No wonder it had given him a shock. I'd hit him as hard as I could. The class sat there as though the school had been struck by lightning, our old caretaker was standing by the blackboard looking as stupid as possible, and the electric sparks were sparking for all they were worth. But nobody was taking any notice of them.

" 'Who was that?' said Kaul, after a long pause.

" 'I, sir,' I said. 'I beg your pardon, sir, I didn't mean to hurt you.'

" 'Well, you did,' he said. And then he stalked out of the room in the middle of the lesson, holding his head as though he was afraid it would fall off."

"Great!" said Pony. "What a one you are!"

Gustav thought for a moment. "I didn't care what happened then. The others were sitting there scared to death, and I got hold of Mehnert and lammed him till his clothes wouldn't fit. He was absent for three days. When I'd finished with Mehnert they took me off to the head. Kaul was sitting on his sofa with a cold compress on the back of his neck.

" 'It has just come to my ears that you have assaulted in the dark an old and respected member of the staff of this school,' began the head. 'We shall, of course, have to expel you. But first I must ask you to explain the reasons for this treacherous attack.' That was a nasty one for me. Nobody had ever called me treacherous. So I told them the whole story. I said if anybody was treacherous it was their model boy Mehnert. And the punishment had been meant for him because he'd gone sneaking off in the long break telling tales to the head. And if they liked they could go to the physics lab and look at the remains of their favourite pupil. If they thought chaps like him were better than me, that was their look-out. And so on."

Captain Schmauch looked affectionately at the angry Gustav. "And what happened then?"

"Then old Kaul did something I shall never forget to the end of my days."

"What did he do?" asked Emil.

"He laughed," said Gustav. "He laughed till the compress dropped off the back of his neck."

Captain Schmauch slapped his knee again. Then he turned to the waiter, who was still standing nearby listening to the story. "Waiter, another grog! And a picture post-card. Hurry up!"

"Who have you suddenly decided to write a card to?" asked Emil's grandmother.

"I know," said Emil.

"Well, who then?" asked the captain, smiling.

"Herr Kaul, the physics master."

"Quite right," said Captain Schmauch. "He deserves one."

Chapter 7

CABARET IN KORLSBÜTTEL

The orchestra struck up. Then a rather over-dressed man appeared on the stage and conveyed to the audience, which had appeared in such goodly numbers, the compliments of the management. He promised them a pleasant evening, and proceeded to make a few wisecracks at which no one laughed but himself. That seemed to annoy him and he soon announced the first turn: "Ferdinand Badstübner, the Caruso with the lute."

Caruso Badstübner was a stout, grey-haired man with a bass-lute in his hand and a student's cap on his head. He twanged the strings and sang several songs, dealing mainly with Heidelberg, sweethearts, lovely inn-keepers' daughters and large numbers of wine-barrels and beer-mugs. His voice did not sound quite new. When he had finished he waved his little cap and the curtain fell.

"They can't have had much time left for their studies, can they?" said the Professor to his father.

"These songs are so exaggerated," returned Herr Haberland. "If they hadn't worked they would never have learnt anything."

Klotilde also had a question to ask. "How comes it that that elderly man who has just been singing is still a student? And if he's really a student why is he on the stage singing songs?"

They looked at each other. At last Emil's grandmother said: "He's probably a student of music."

"I see," said Klotilde Seelenbinder. "That explains it, of course."

And she could not understand why the others should laugh.

"I'm not going to college," said Gustav. "I'm going to be a racing-motorist or a stunt-airman." He turned to Emil. "What about you?"

Emil shut his eyes for a moment. He was thinking of Herr Jeschke and their talk. "No," he answered. "I'm not going to college either. I want to make some money as soon as I can, and be independent."

His grandmother looked at him through the corner of her eye but said nothing.

The next performer was an acrobatic danseuse. She spun round so quickly on her own axis that sometimes you had an impression that her eyes were in the back of her head and the nape of her neck was where her face ought to be.

The captain clapped his big hands so hard

that it sounded as though he were bursting blown-up paper bags. He leaned towards Klotilde: "Can you dance like that?" he asked.

But he had come to the wrong address. "I should be ashamed," she answered, "to perform such antics before strangers."

"Well, you might perform them at home one day," the Professor suggested. And the boys chuckled at the thought of Fräulein See-lenbinder, sometimes called Schlips, per-forming the hand-stand on the veranda of "Seaside Villa" when she ought to have been cooking the dinner.

Then the orchestra played dance-music. Some people danced, among them Captain Schmauch. He danced with Klotilde. And Herr Haberland with his wife. Emil's grand-mother wagged her head to the music and smiled happily.

Suddenly a young man came up and

bowed to Pony Hütchen. "May I have the honour, Fräulein?" he asked.

Emil looked at him with a smile. "She hasn't learnt to dance yet," he said.

Pony rose to her feet. "A lot you know, my lad!" And she danced off with the young man as though she had been doing nothing else all her life.

"Well, just look at our Fräulein," said the Professor. "And she's never had a single lesson!"

"We girls have dancing in our bones," said her grandmother.

Gustav shook his head. "A kid like that!" he said disgustedly. "No older than me and pretends to be a young lady!"

The next dance was a waltz. "That's for us young people," remarked the captain to Pony. And he danced off with her so vigorously that the rest of the dancers thought it wiser to retire. Sometimes he swung Pony high in the air. It was a marvellous exhibition.

When they had finished there was loud applause. Even from the waiters. The captain whispered to Pony that she was to curtsy. Then he made a curtsy himself.

Presently the overdressed man appeared on the stage again. It was with special pleasure, he said, that he introduced an artiste who had been received with the loudest applause in the most famous cabarets of Germany.

"That's very odd," said Captain Schmauch. "If he's so successful why does he come here of all places?" They waited curiously for the curtain to rise.

And when it rose and the famous artiste stood revealed, Emil exclaimed audibly: "Why, it's only him."

The great artiste was none other than the compère himself, equipped with a silk hat, a walking-stick and a monocle.

"Here I am!" he cried. "My first number will be a serious song entitled 'That's How

Life Is'. Theobald, let her have it!" (By Theobald he meant the pianist, and by "her" the piano.)

When he had finished, Emil's grandmother declared: "If that jackanapes has appeared in the most famous cabarets of Germany, I'm the Grand Duchess of Neustadt."

The performer proceeded to sing two comic songs which were just as lugubrious as the one that had preceded them. Then he announced that there would be an interval of ten minutes.

The boys left the hotel, went on to the dunes and looked at the sea. It was smooth and leaden; only the reflection of the moon ran across it like a narrow silver path. The waves broke at regular intervals on the shore. The silhouettes of bathing tents stood out against the sky like stacked corn in a dark field.

All this, beneath a sky studded with glittering stars, was a little uncanny.

"I feel cold," said the Professor in a low voice.

They re-entered the hotel, and sat down with Pony and the grown-ups.

After the interval the acrobatic danseuse made another appearance. She was followed by a conjurer, who did extraordinary tricks with playing cards, and then came the star-turn of the evening – the Three Byrons.

The things Mr. Byron managed to do with his twins were hardly credible. The spectators sat motionless on their seats, scarcely daring to breathe. It began to reach its climax when Mr. Byron lay on his back on a tabouret and held up his hands. Jackie, the taller of the twins, then stood on his head in the palm of his father's right hand while Mackie did the same in the palm of his left. At first they steadied themselves by holding Mr. Byron's arms, but presently they loosed their hold and put their hands straight at their sides.

They stood on their heads thus like little inverted soldiers. Then they jumped down, landed on their feet and smiled as though nothing had happened.

Mr. Byron, still on his tabouret, drew up his knees and put both legs straight up in the air. Mackie lay down with his stomach on the soles of his father's feet. Then Mr. Byron began to move his feet almost as though he were pedalling a bicycle and Mackie began to revolve rapidly round his own axis. Suddenly he flew into the air, turned over and over, came down on Byron's feet, was again thrown upward, turned through an angle of ninety degrees and fell – no, that is the wrong word – alighted with his feet firmly planted on those of his father.

"I daren't look at any more," said Klotilde in a trembling voice.

But Emil, Gustav and the Professor were swept off their feet with enthusiasm.

"What a pity Little Tuesday isn't here!" said Gustav.

Then Jackie Byron lay down on the tabouret, held up his arms and took hold of his father's hands. And that tall, burly acrobat performed the hand-stand on his son's upraised arms!

"It's a wonder that Jackie's bones can stand it!" whispered Emil.

Gustav nodded. "It's against all the laws of physics."

When the Three Byrons had finished their turn, a storm of applause broke out. The natives of Korlsbüttel, who had been standing outside the hotel watching through the gaps in the curtains, clapped and clapped till the bats fluttered excitedly around their heads. The Byron family took twelve curtain-calls.

Gustav grasped his English dictionary and rose from his seat, resolved to do or die.

Suddenly he flew into the air

"Come on!" he said, as he hurried off. Emil and the Professor hastily followed.

They waited in the corridor behind the stage till the twins came out.

"Hello boys," cried the Professor in English.

The twins turned round.

"A moment, please," said Gustav.

Mackie, the smaller of the two, trotted off and disappeared into a back room. Jackie stopped.

"You are wonderful," said Emil. "Very nice indeed. My compliments, Byron."

Jackie Byron turned and came up to them. He looked frightfully tired and hot.

Gustav hunted through his dictionary. "Hello, dear!" he stammered. "We have seen you. It is the greatest impression in all my life, by Jove! Do you understand?"

Jackie Byron looked from one to the other.

"Don't be such silly chumps," he said in a low voice. "I don't know a word of English!"

The three boys looked at him in astonishment.

Gustav shut his dictionary with a bang. "What a sell! I thought you were an Englishman."

"No fear!" said Jackie. "Byron's only our stage name. Foreign names always sound better. What do you think my real name is?"

They frowned and thought hard. "You'd better tell us," said the Professor. "Or we shall have to guess our way through the telephone directory."

Jackie put one finger to his lips. "Promise you won't tell a soul! My name . . . no, it's a secret."

"My name's Tischbein," volunteered Emil. "Yours couldn't be much worse than that."

"It could," said Jackie. "All right. My name's Paul Pachulke, and I come from Teltow."

"Paul Pachulke," repeated Gustav in an awed voice. "From Teltow, where the turnips come from." He was dumbfounded. "Well, it's not all that important. My name's Gustav. And we wanted to tell you that we think you're just marvellous. Gosh! You're in a class by yourself."

Jackie was much pleased with this high praise. "It's very decent of you," he said. "Shall you be on the shore again in the morning?"

They nodded.

"Then I'll see you there." And he ran off into the room which his brother had previously entered.

The three friends stood in the corridor looking at each other. At last they could not help laughing.

Gustav rammed his dictionary contemptuously into his pocket, and took Emil and the Professor by the arm. "There you are," he said. "And that's what we learn foreign languages for!"

Chapter 8

THE THIRD TWIN APPEARS

Next day it rained cats and dogs. They stayed in the house, wrote letters and postcards, played chess and draughts, frequently looked out of the window, and felt like worms in a sand-pit. Happily Little Tuesday came to see them. He looked like a mushroom as he stood at the door beneath his father's umbrella.

They let him in and gushed to him at great length about the Three Byrons and their feats. They also told him that Pony Hütchen had been addressed as "Fräulein".

"Ah, we're getting old," said Tuesday.

Pony was in the kitchen, taking a cookery lesson with Klotilde, so they ran down the passage and threw open the kitchen-door. "Fräulein," they called, "your dancing-partner is outside."

And Pony actually looked out of the window.

The boys laughed and ran back to the veranda. "I've got to write an essay about what I did in the holidays," said the Professor. "I suppose you chaps have too."

"Rather!" said Gustav. "It's always the same. The pleasantest thing that happened to me, or the most exciting, or the most interesting. You get to a point when you don't want anything to happen at all."

"If this beastly weather's going on, we might as well write the essay today," the Professor proposed. "Then it will be over and done with."

Emil was in favour, but Gustav and Tuesday were against.

The Professor tried to effect a compromise. "We could at least make some notes." He fetched from the table a book that belonged to his father and turned over the pages. "Perhaps there's something in here . . . a quotation at any rate."

"Our German master hates quotations," said Gustav. "He says we ought to think of what to say for ourselves, instead of copying it out of books. He says it's just as bad as copying from your neighbour." He laughed quietly. "I prefer to copy from my neighbour."

Emil asked the Professor what he was reading.

"I shan't tell you," said the Professor. "You must guess. Listen to this!" He sat down on the table and read aloud: "Among us song is the first step in training the young; the way is thus prepared for all else. The simplest

157

enjoyment and the simplest lesson are enliv-
ened and impressed upon the mind by means
of song, yes, even the traditions handed down
in the form of belief or custom are communi-
cated through song." The Professor looked
up. "Well, who wrote that?"

"The conductor of a choral society, I
should think," said Gustav.

The Professor laughed. "Wrong. My word,
you've dropped a brick. It was Goethe."

"If it was Goethe, Professor," said Tuesday, "it was *von* Goethe. He was a member
of the nobility."

"It's not all that important," muttered
Gustav.

The Professor went on reading: "By training children to write signs on a blackboard
to represent the musical sounds they make,
and then, on reading these signs, to repro-
duce the sounds in their throats, and finally
to write the text beneath them, we teach
them to develop simultaneously hand, ear,

and eye, and they thus learn more quickly than one would expect to write accurately and neatly. Finally, since all this must be practised and copied by strict measure and by exact numbers, they grasp the high value of the arts of measuring and calculating much more quickly than in any other way. We have therefore chosen music among all conceivable alternatives as the foundation of our education, for the paths that run there-from are equally clearly trodden in all directions."

"Was von Goethe a schoolmaster then?" asked Tuesday in surprise. "I thought he was a politician."

"All singing!" cried Gustav in disgust. "Just imagine what it would be like if we had to sing simple interest and equations. I can't see the sense of it."

"Goethe must have meant only the first years at school," said Emil. "All the subjects are closely connected in the elementary stages."

Just then Herr Haberland came in. "What are you reading?" he asked.

His son told him.

"Oh," said Herr Haberland. "*Wilhelm Meister*."

"I'm all against having to sing lessons," declared Gustav. "I always get bad marks in singing because I haven't got a musical ear. Just think what would happen if I had to sing every lesson and every subject . . . Latin, maths, history, and so on. I daren't think of it."

"I don't suppose you're much good at Latin and maths even without the singing," said Tuesday.

"How on earth did you guess?" asked Gustav. "You're quite right. Well, I don't care if we have to conjugate irregular verbs as four-part songs."

Herr Haberland laughed. "The branch of

pedagogics which Goethe describes in this book is the humanistic ideal of a very old and very great writer. You will understand it better later on."

"It's not hard to understand," said the Professor. "Listen to this!" And he read: "Healthy, well-born children bring much with them at birth; nature has given them all they need for the present and future. Our duty is to develop it; it often develops better when left to itself."

He closed the book and looked round at his friends. "There you have it."

"What?" asked Gustav. "We are all healthy, well-born children. What about it?"

The Professor tapped the book with his forefinger. "Goethe means . . ."

"*Von* Goethe means," corrected Tuesday.

"Goethe means that we have by nature, still hidden as it were, all that we need for life. He means that it can develop itself. There's no need for someone to be always

161

doctoring at us with regulations and supervision and criticism." He looked across at his father. "Of course you know that I don't mean you, Daddy. But many parents and teachers tackle the thing in the wrong way."

"It's confoundedly hard," said Herr Haberland, "to avoid training children either too much or too little, and the problem is different with every child. One develops his inherent abilities smoothly and another has to have them dragged out of him with a pair of forceps, or they would never come to light at all." He sat down. "You'll find it out when you have children of your own."

"I'm looking forward to that," said Emil.

"Well," said Herr Haberland. "Sometimes it's enough to turn your hair grey!" He looked across at his son. "You know I don't mean you, old man."

"I'm beginning to understand that idea of developing yourself," declared Gustav. "I'm sure I could become just as good a racing-motorist without dictation and detentions and reports. In fact a jolly sight better! I should have more time for practice."

"Well, boys," said Herr Haberland with a smile, "would you like to have a few days to develop yourselves in peace? You can, if you like. I noticed in the window of a travel-bureau a poster announcing a few days' trip to Copenhagen, starting the day after tomorrow. I haven't been in Copenhagen for a long time, nor in Klampenburg and Marienlyst. It's about time I went to Denmark again, and I propose to take my wife, Emil's grand-mother, our Klotilde and Pony Hütchen. We shall leave Warnemünde the day after to-morrow."

"And what about us?" asked the Professor.

"You boys will stay behind in Korlsbüttel. You can take your midday meal at the inn. I'll leave you some money, that is provided you don't regard it as too great an infringement of your liberty."

"We won't be mean," said Gustav. "We'll take the money."

"But you must look after the rest for yourselves," said Herr Haberland. "That will give you plenty of opportunity to develop as much as you like. You will be responsible to yourselves alone and you'll find out whether that's a pleasure or a burden. What do you say?"

The boys accepted the proposal with enthusiasm.

The Professor went up to his father. "Could anyone have a better father than mine?" he asked proudly.

"No!" they shouted.

Little Tuesday put up his hand as though he were in class. "Herr Haberland," he said, "couldn't you take my parents along with you?"

In the afternoon it was still raining. They were sitting at coffee when Captain Schmauch looked in. Klotilde had to make him a glass of stiff grog. He sat down in the armchair, filled his pipe and puffed blue clouds of smoke into the curtains. "It's cosy here," he said. "Since we were all together last night I've been quite lonely in my own house."

"You should have got married when you were a young man," remarked Emil's grandmother.

"No," said the captain. "It's not right for the husband to be at sea, and the wife always sitting at home by herself. That's no good. I'm off again tonight for a day or two, going to the south coast of Sweden for a cargo of timber. That's how it's been for years. Always alone! It wouldn't be so bad if Hans would stay in Korlsbüttel. But when he's finished his apprenticeship at the hotel, he'll be off to England and France. A waiter must have travelled about a bit. He can't stay at home for the sake of an old uncle. Well, well, you get older and older till one fine day you've got to the end of things." He was quite touched, so they gave him another glass of grog.

Then he had to go on board. He put on his oilskin coat and tramped off through the rain, making for Sweden.

After supper the boys were sitting on the veranda again. Tuesday was still there. He had his parents' permission to stay till nine. The rain pattered on the glass roof. They were feeling bored.

Suddenly a face appeared outside the glass, and they heard a faint tapping.

The four boys sprang to their feet. The Professor ran to the door and threw it open. "Who's there?"

A muffled figure slipped in.

It was Hans Schmauch, the piccolo. "Sorry to disturb you," he said. "But I need your advice." He threw off his wet coat. "Listen to this," he continued. "About eight o'clock Mr. Byron ordered a cup of tea to be brought up to his own room. So I took it up, and was on the point of leaving when he said he had something to ask me, but I was not to mention it to a soul. I nodded. What else could I do? Then he said: 'You're a first-rate gymnast. I've seen you on the bars out there on the shore. You've got talent. If I train you, you'll become a famous acrobat. And besides, you're so wonderfully small and light. Let me lift you!' He lifted me up with one hand and swung me round and round in the air till I hardly knew where I was. Then he put me down again. 'Your tea's getting cold, Mr. Byron,' I said, and went towards the door. But he would not let me go. He asked if I would like to become an acrobat and work with him on the stage. 'But you've got your two twins,' I said. 'What do you want with a third?' 'I don't want a third,' he answered. 'I want a second.' And do you know what he said then?"

The boys listened intently.

EMIL AND THE THREE TWINS

Mr. Byron ordered a cup of tea

"It sounded so odd," went on the piccolo, "and yet so sinister. He said: 'Jackie's getting too heavy for me.' "

"Too heavy?" repeated Tuesday.

"Yes. Jackie's growing. And the taller he grows the heavier he weighs. He's got so heavy that his father's had to give up some of the tricks he used to do with him. And other things don't work properly, or they're getting too dangerous. If Jackie goes on growing, Mr. Byron won't be able to perform with him at all."

The boys stood there in silence.

"And so Mr. Byron wants me to go away with him and Mackie," went on the piccolo. "He wants to slip off with us one night without Jackie knowing a word about it. Mr. Byron said he wasn't likely to find another boy like me in a hurry."

Emil slapped his forehead. "But good heavens!" he cried. "The man can't leave his own son high and dry because the boy's growing. That's absolute nonsense! What would become of Jackie?"

"Poor old Paul!" said Gustav to himself.

The Professor was pacing up and down. "That's a fine idea! We can't possibly allow him to act like that. Simply throw one twin overboard and engage another in his place? It's out of the question."

"It's a good thing the grown-ups are off to Denmark," declared Gustav. "They won't be able to get in our way."

Emil banged the table. "We'll give old Hercules the surprise of his life! This is a job for us detectives." He turned to the piccolo. "When is he proposing to steal away?"

"That depends entirely on me," returned Hans Schmauch. "I'm a chance that'll never turn up again, he says."

"We'll wait till our old people have gone. Then we'll hold a council of war straight away," said the Professor. "Now listen, Hans,

170

you must keep putting Byron off until we're ready. Understand?"

The piccolo nodded.

"But I'm not going to be at the telephone this time," said Tuesday. "So now you know."

"There'll be no telephoning at all this time," said Gustav. "It will all be direct action."

Hans Schmauch put on his wet coat. "Then you'll let me know?" He went to the door. "Password Emil!" He was gone.

"Password Emil!" they shouted after him.

The only answer was the howling of the wind.

Suddenly the inner door opened and Klotilde Seelenbinder put her head into the room. "What was the matter?"

"My dear Schlips," returned the Professor. "What *are* you talking about?"

Chapter 9

DETECTIVES AMONG THEMSELVES

Two mornings later the adults set off with Pony for Warnemünde to board the boat for Denmark. At the last moment, the women-folk, especially Klotilde, who was terribly excited, wanted to give the boys a thousand bits of advice on domestic matters, but Herr Haberland bundled them into the compartment and handed twenty marks to the Professor. "Don't forget to take your midday meal at the inn. Anything else you want you can get at Warkentien's store. There are

172

plenty of reserve rations in Klotilde's pantry. Mind you lock the doors carefully at night, and don't get up to any foolishness. If anything happens that you can't deal with yourselves, telegraph to Copenhagen. We shall be at the Hotel d'Angleterre."

"There'll be no need to telegraph," said the Professor.

"All the better," returned his father. "And a happy course of self-development to all of you." Then he got into the railway-carriage. The women looked out of the window and waved their hands.

A few minutes later, Emil, Gustav and the Professor were alone, and there was nothing to obstruct their independent development.

They went back to the house. The weather was dull and the wind had a chill edge to it. Bathing was out of the question.

The Professor fetched paper and pencil from the desk, and settled his spectacles comfortably on his nose. "First of all," he said, "we must plan out our work. Every day one of us will be on duty. I today, Emil tomorrow, and Gustav the day after. The work will consist of waking the others, running errands, making coffee, getting supper, locking up, and doing anything else that's needed."

"But each man will clean his own teeth," said Gustav, and giggled foolishly. Then he grew serious and said that he could not make coffee.

"You'll learn," replied Emil. Thereupon they went to the pantry and conscientiously took stock. They made a careful note of the number of eggs, tins of meat, sausages, potatoes, pickled cucumbers, apples, loaves, packets of butter and dripping, and so forth.

"The old people will be surprised when they see how well we've managed," declared the Professor. Then, since he was on duty, he took a string bag and went off to Warkentien's to do some shopping. Emil and Gustav went with him.

They looked round Warkentien's shop for some time and the proprietor recommended all kinds of things. The Professor looked nervously at his two companions. Then he said to the shopkeeper: "I'm sorry to have troubled you, Herr Warkentien, but I think we've got all we need at home in the pantry." Then they set off again with the empty string bag.

"That's something," said the Professor, as they entered the house, "that a man has to learn by experience."

"Hm!" grunted Gustav. He picked up an apple and took a large bite.

The Professor reached for the stock-list and crossed out one apple. "You must keep things in order," he remarked.

"Not all that important," mumbled Gustav with his mouth full.

When they were about to set out for the inn for their midday meal, Emil said: "You know we could save that money. I'll tell you what . . . I'll cook!"

"What are you going to cook?" inquired Gustav.

"You'll see," said Emil and rolled up his shirt sleeves. "We've got eggs and butter and sausage. I'll fry some sausage and eggs together. We can fill up with bread and have some tinned strawberries to finish with."

He put on one of Klotilde's aprons, placed on the table a knife, butter, eggs, sausage and salt, put the frying pan on the gas-cooker, dropped a nub of butter into the pan, put slices of sausage in the sizzling fat, broke two eggs on the edge of the pan, poured their contents skilfully over the sausage and sprinkled a bit of salt on the whole mixture.

His friends followed these complex operations with interest and silent admiration.

"I didn't let the yolks break," said Emil proudly. "That's the hardest part."

Suddenly Little Tuesday looked in through the kitchen-window. He swung himself on to the sill and squatted down there comfortably, watching Emil. "Like a professional cook," he said approvingly.

"It's all practice," answered Emil. "You see, we haven't a servant, and if my mother's busy at dinner-time I have to see to the meal myself."

Tuesday told them he had obtained permission to spend the next few nights at the Professor's house. The friends were delighted. "But," added Tuesday, "my people refuse point-blank to go to Copenhagen. They say they don't want to . . . as if that was a reason!"

"Stubborn!" said Gustav, disgustedly.

Tuesday shrugged his shoulders. "And then you're expected to go in for independent development!"

Emil turned down the gas. "We can't all eat at once. What's in the frying pan is for Gustav, because he's the greediest." They laughed, all except Gustav. "You loobies!" he said. He had invented the expression himself.

The Professor fetched a plate and a knife and fork from the dresser. Emil coaxed the fried eggs on to the plate and cut two slices of bread. "Take your seats for the first luncheon," he cried. "Here you are, sir, before it gets cold."

Gustav sat down at the kitchen-table, crumbled the bread over the eggs and began to tuck in.

The Professor fetched a kitchen towel and they tied it round Gustav's neck. He looked as though he were at the dentist's. Emil put the second portion of sausage and eggs into the frying pan.

The Professor sat down on a bench. "Now we must get to business," he said. "While Emil and I are having our dinner and washing up the things, Gustav and Tuesday will go to the Strand Hotel and get in touch with Hans Schmauch. First we must know whether Mr. Byron still wants to run away with him. If so, Hans is to discuss it all with Mr. Byron, and find out when they are going and whether by train or boat."

"I could lend them my motor-bike," said Gustav sarcastically. "But I don't see why we should let the chap make all his preparations. Why not go to him and tell him not to make an ass of himself? Say he's got to stay here or he'll be up against us. That would be much simpler."

"No, it wouldn't," declared Emil. "If we did that he'd stay here for a day or two and then carry out his plans just the same. And even if he didn't take Hans with him, he'd leave Jackie behind."

"That's right," said the Professor. "You must do as I proposed."

"And tell Hans Schmauch," added Emil,

"that he's to arrange matters so that they plan to leave late in the evening."

"Why?" asked Tuesday.

"Because Jackie will be asleep and will know nothing of his father's treachery. When he wakes up next morning his father and Mackie will have come back, and he will have been saved all the disappointment."

Gustav rose from the table. "Those were the best fried eggs I've ever tasted. Keep me a plate of strawberries, you two kitchen-maids." He pushed little Tuesday off the window-sill into the garden and vaulted after him.

Emil and the Professor heard their footsteps as they ran down the gravel path, and then the slam of the garden gate.

The two boys finished their meal and put aside a plate of strawberries for Gustav. Then they went to the sink and while Emil washed up, the Professor wiped the crockery and put it back on the dresser.

The frying pan took the most cleaning, but at last they could see their faces in it.

They washed their hands. "Fathers seem to be a source of trouble," said Emil as he hung the towel on the nail. "One boy's father wants to desert him, and another boy is to have a step-father foisted on him when he doesn't want one."

"Which other boy?" asked the Professor. When Emil said nothing in reply he looked at him, and suddenly he understood.

"I've not spoken to anyone about it yet," said Emil in a low voice, "not even to my mother. But, of course, she's the last one I could talk to about it."

"I won't tell a soul," said the Professor.

Emil unhooked the frying pan from one nail and hung it on another. He turned off the water-tap a little more tightly. He closed the window. "I must tell someone. I'm in a

181

pretty rotten position, you see. I can hardly remember my father. My mother and I have been alone together for so long, and it never even occurred to me that that might change. I always thought how grand it would be when I was earning my own living. I thought we could choose whether to go away in the holidays or stay at home; and do whichever we liked. Then we could take a bigger flat, with good furniture and plenty of good books. And we could have a charwoman twice a week and send the washing to the laundry. Well, that's the sort of thing I looked forward to. And now a man has come along and wants to marry my mother. Who'll take the bigger flat now? . . . He. Who'll go away for holidays with her? . . . He. And who'll pay for the charwoman? . . . He. He earns the money. And it doesn't matter whether I earn any or not. I can even go to college, he says. He's always at our house. And it's quite impossible now for me to tell mother everything. Sometimes I think she's not even interested any more. And I can't go to sleep at night. And when she comes in I breathe deeply to make her think I'm asleep. And all the time I feel I should like to cry like a first-form kid." Emil swallowed hard. Then he exerted all his strength and pulled himself together. "Well, it'll come out all right. If she loves him, of course she must marry him."

"Does she love him?"

"What do you think? Why should she marry him if she didn't? She *must* love him. He's a decent sort and all that. He and I get on very well together." He looked at his friend. "What do *you* think about it?"

"I think you are too egoistic," said the Professor. "Don't you? After all, your mother is not only your mother, she's a woman. Since your father's death she's forgotten that point in looking after you. You were small and needed her. But now you're big and she's beginning to think of herself again."

"I tell myself that a hundred times a day. I'm not so egoistic. Only somehow it's such an awful pity."

"Many things in life are an awful pity," said the Professor. "But you and I can't change them. It's much better for you to be disappointed than your mother. Isn't it?"

"Yes," said Emil. "But you can see now how glad I was to get your invitation. I'm not good at pretending. She would probably have seen through me. And if she had she would have turned him down straight off. She told him right at the beginning that she would only marry him if I approved. And he had to ask me."

"Jolly decent of her," said the Professor, admiringly.

"Well," said Emil. "What do you expect? She's my mother!"

They put on their coats and went out to

find their two friends. They met them in the alder-coppice.

"It's all fixed for tomorrow night," reported Gustav. "You see, tomorrow is Hans Schmauch's day off, and this chap Byron will slip away in the evening with Hans and the junior twin. Hans wants us to tell him what he's to do. That Byron has made up his mind to go by the last steamer, so that he won't need to leave the hotel till Jackie's asleep. At Warnemünde he'll take the train for Poland. He has relations there and he wants to practise with his new twin before taking another engagement."

"I've got a very simple plan," said Tuesday. "We'll all line up at the landing-stage, and when he comes we'll make him go back to bed."

The Professor shook his head. "That's too simple. We must let him get properly started before we catch him; otherwise he'll simply make some excuse. Unless he's already gone

185

some distance he'll simply laugh in our faces. He's got to be afraid that we shall alarm the harbour police."

They sat down on a bench provided by the local Improvement Society, and discussed the problem for half an hour. At the end of that time their plan was complete. The piccolo was to inform Mr. Byron that he could not go aboard with him and Mackie in Korlsbüttel. He, Hans Schmauch, would board the steamer at its next stopping-place, that is, at Heidekrug.

"And how is Hans to get to Heidekrug?" asked Gustav.

"How do you think?" cried Emil. "On the back of your motor-bike, of course."

"I see," said Gustav.

"The detectives, on the other hand," said the Professor, "will not board the steamer in Heidekrug with Hans Schmauch, nor in Korlsbüttel with Mr. Byron and Mackie, but at a still earlier stopping-place, namely at

Graal. We shall go down below and at Korlsbüttel we shall keep watch to see whether old Byron really comes aboard. In Heidekrug the piccolo will join him, and shortly before we get to Warnemünde we shall go up on deck and tackle Byron. 'Here, Herr Pachulke,' we shall say. 'What have you done with your son Paul? And how comes the piccolo to be travelling with you in his place? If you don't want to be handed over to the police in Warnemünde for deserting your son and abducting Hans Schmauch, you had better come back with us to Korlsbüttel, either by train or in a taxi at your own expense. We don't want Jackie to know anything of all this.' Well, do you think he'll give us any trouble?"

"He'll have to come back to Korlsbüttel," cried Tuesday triumphantly, "whether he wants to or not."

"That's all very fine," said Gustav. "But how will the detectives get to Graal?"

They all looked at him reproachfully.

"I see," said Gustav. "On the back of my motor-bike."

"That's right," said Emil. "You'll have to ride to and fro till all the detectives are at Graal. And then you'll ride alone from Graal through Korlsbüttel and Heidekrug to Warnemünde and find out the nearest post of the harbour police. Just in case Mr. Byron tries to give any trouble. When the steamer comes in, you'll be there waiting for us and the prisoner. Do you see?"

"I do," returned Gustav. "But what about my motor-bike?"

Chapter 10

ADVENTURE BY LAND AND WATER

The next day was Tuesday. Emil was on duty, and when he opened the outer door to take in the milk and the rolls he stood as if rooted to the spot. Hans Schmauch, the piccolo, was sitting outside in the grass. "Good morning," he said, laughing. "It's my day off today, and I've got to make the most of it."

"Why didn't you ring the bell?"

"Not I! I work in an hotel, and I know what a bore it is to be fetched out of bed by a bell ringing. Besides it was so nice and peaceful here in the grass. The grass is going up."

They went into the kitchen and made the coffee. While they were doing so, Emil explained the plan the detectives had thought out the evening before. "I'll run over the chief points again," he said, when he had finished. "We detectives shall board the boat in Graal, Byron and Mackie here in Korlsbüttel and you in Heidekrug. Gustav will be waiting with his motor-bike by the landing-stage at Warnemünde. If Byron resists, Gustav will fetch the police, while we others hold on to him."

Hans Schmauch found the plan an excellent one. They laid the breakfast-table and wakened their friends. They called Little Tuesday "Fräulein" because he had been sleeping in Pony's room.

The piccolo hung a napkin over his arm and waited on them with professional skill.

"Just like a real head-waiter," remarked

Gustav approvingly. "Another glass of milk please, waiter."

"Certainly, sir," said Hans Schmauch. He dashed into the kitchen, returned adroitly balancing a glass of milk on a tray, and put it down in front of Gustav. "Do you propose to stay here long, sir? The weather looks like improving, and this hotel is excellently conducted. I'm sure you will be most comfortable here, sir."

"I'm very sorry," returned Gustav. "I must get back to Berlin immediately. I shut my wife and children in the wardrobe by mistake and locked the door."

"That's a pity," said Hans Schmauch. "Otherwise you would have been able to see the film *Emil and the Detectives* in our local cinema next Friday."

"What?" they cried, springing to their feet.

The piccolo took a page of a newspaper from his pocket and fastened it to a picture-

191

frame. Among the advertisements was a particularly large one with the following text:

EMIL AND THE DETECTIVES
A FILM WITH TWO HUNDRED CHILDREN!
FOUNDED ON FACT!
BREATH-TAKING EXCITEMENT!
A STORY OF CONTEMPORARY BERLIN!
A FILM FOR CHILDREN FROM EIGHT TO EIGHTY.
FRIDAY NEXT AT
THE LIGHTHOUSE CINEMA.

They read the advertisement over and over again. Gustav swaggered up and down, shouting: "Walk up, walk up, ladies and gentlemen! Here you will see the cleverest boys of the age! Come inside! You'll laugh till you split."

"It's only a film," said the Professor, "and we're not even playing in it, but I've got stage-fright."

"No one will know we're in the audience,"

Emil reassured him. "Unless you've gone and split on us, Hans."

"Not a word!" said the piccolo. "You're all incognito." Suddenly he slapped his forehead. "Where's my memory? I came to take you out for a sail. That's why I got up so early. Let's go out for the day and take food and everything. We'll get back here late this afternoon."

"I shall stay here," declared Emil. "I'm on duty."

"What rot!" exclaimed Gustav. "No one's going to run away with a house. Come along, you!"

"There's plenty of room in the boat," said the piccolo. "And there's a dinghy too."

But Emil stuck to his word.

"I can't come either," said Tuesday. "I've got to be back to have lunch with my people or there'll be an awful row. They'll probably forbid me to sleep here. And then I shouldn't be able to take part in the expedition against

Mr. Byron. Last time I had to stick by the telephone and missed everything. It would just about finish me if I missed the fun again."

"All right," said Gustav. "Then we three'll go. I don't know the first thing about sailing, so I shall look after the motor if we use it."

"Trust me!" said Hans Schmauch. "I'll tell you what to do."

They ran off to the kitchen and the Professor distributed the provisions for the picnic. They packed it all into an old market-basket: apples, tinned fruit, sausage, bread, butter, knives, forks, plates and napkins. Emil, who was on duty, made a note of each item on the stock-list.

Gustav picked up the full basket. "I'll carry this. Food wants careful handling."

"It's not all that important," said Emil, laughing.

"Grub's one of the things *that* doesn't

apply to," said Gustav emphatically. "Honour where honour is due."

Then they set off for the harbour.

"Be back punctually!" shouted Emil as they started up the motor. "We've got a big job in front of us!"

"Password Emil!" cried Gustav, sitting down at the wheel.

"He's eating another apple," said Tuesday to Emil. Then he shouted to the boys in the boat: "Password Emil!"

The boat threaded its way out of the harbour. Hans Schmauch was standing by the mast, hoisting the mainsail.

The Professor put on his beret and waved his hand. The boat slipped past the end of the landing-stage into the open sea. A light breeze was blowing.

"They've switched off the motor now," said Tuesday. Emil nodded, shaded his eyes with his hands and looked after his comrades.

Hans Schmauch had set the foresail. The boat was moving north-west.

"Ahoy!" yelled Little Tuesday.

About this time the visitors to Denmark were sitting on the terrace of the Industrie Restaurant in Copenhagen. They were eating their breakfast and listening appreciatively to the wonderful peal of bells in the tower of the Town Hall. They were also studying with admiration the appetites of their neighbours.

"The smaller the country, the bigger the appetites of its inhabitants," declared Herr Haberland.

Emil's grandmother was watching a Dane and his wife at the next table. "It's a miracle," she exclaimed. "Just think of the amount of food those two people have eaten since we came here! They ought to have burst by now or fallen dead from their chairs!"

The two Danes were not to be disturbed.

The waiter was just serving them with the next course.

"Cooks must have a busy time here," reflected Fräulein Seelenbinder. "I think I'm better off with you, ma'am."

Frau Haberland smiled. "I'm glad we're both so satisfied with each other," she said.

Klotilde blushed and made no reply.

Pony Hütchen sat with her head bent over a notebook she had wisely brought with her. She was writing down all that had happened to her since she arrived in Copenhagen. Her notes were very briefly expressed. "Gedser," she wrote, and "Fireship. Vivel, lovely supper. Tivoli, a great big fair. Amalienborg. Christiansborg. Old Bourse, marvellous gabled front. Foreign warships, even Japanese. Long line, crowded shore by harbour. Thorwaldsen Museum."

"I wonder how the boys are getting on now?" said Klotilde.

"They're glad to be rid of us," said Herr Haberland.

Klotilde Schlips would not believe it.

"I know better," declared Herr Haberland. "I was a boy myself once."

Pony looked at him incredulously.

"Oh yes, I was, Pony," he said, laughing. "I know it's a long time ago, but sometimes I feel as though it were only yesterday." Then he called the waiter, paid the bill, and led the way from the restaurant.

On the Westerbroegade they got into an Überland-omnibus and travelled across the island of Zealand with English, Danish and French tourists. The road led northward, past rows of tidy houses and gardens, and everywhere red climbing roses were in bloom. One very pretty place was called Klampenborg. Pony quickly wrote the name in her notebook.

Sometimes they saw the sea on their right-hand side. It was not really the sea however, but a strait called the Sund. Ocean-going steamers passed through the Sund with bands playing.

And suddenly Pony caught sight of land on the farther side of the Sund. She felt like Columbus as she tugged excitedly at Herr Haberland's sleeve. "What's that over there?" she asked.

"That's Sweden," said Herr Haberland.

"Oh, is it?" cried Pony. Snatching out her notebook, she wrote: "Swedish coast sighted. Herr Haberland awfully nice man."

It was some hours since the sailing-boat *Kunigunde IV* had put out to sea. A light breeze was still blowing. Hans Schmauch had shown the Professor and Gustav how to work the sails, and they were squatting on the weather-side of the boat as it danced merrily across the Baltic Sea. They had already eaten a picnic lunch and everything was as right as right could be. The sun was shining lavishly.

The wind caressed the bronzed faces of the boys as though benevolently disposed towards them.

Gustav lay down on one of the bunks in the little cabin and dreamed he was speeding across the sea on his motor-bike.

Hans Schmauch was steering and the Professor sat at his side, looking down into the sea. Sometimes he saw a bright shimmering jellyfish float by, sometimes a fish.

"What's that?" shouted Hans Schmauch suddenly, and pointed straight ahead.

In front of them lay an island. They turned the boat's head towards it.

"We must go up and take a look at that," said the piccolo.

"It looks like a heap of sand with a bit of grass on it," remarked the Professor.

By this time they were quite close.

"A palm!" cried Hans Schmauch. "A palm in the middle of the Baltic. Who would have believed it?"

"It looks as if it had flu," said the Professor, critically. "It's a fan-palm."

And then the boat gave a sudden jerk.

Hans Schmauch and the Professor were thrown off their seat. Gustav sat up in his bunk and bumped his head against the roof of the cabin. He swore, and crawled out of the cabin. "I suppose we're not sinking?" he asked.

"No," replied Schmauch. "We've grounded."

Gustav examined his environment. "You're a couple of loobies! Couldn't you even steer past a heap of sand? I shouldn't have grumbled if it had been the island of Rügen." He clambered out of the boat. "But it's too jolly careless to run into this weekend plot, when you've got the whole Baltic to sail about in."

"I only wanted to look at the palm," said Schmauch, dejectedly.

"Well, now you can look at it," cried

"A nice outlook!" said Gustav

Gustav. He went up to the alien plant. "A rare specimen, Mr. Naturalist. A palm in a pot. That would be something for Emil, our botanist."

The Professor looked at his watch. "Don't let's mess about! We must be getting back to Korlsbüttel."

They braced themselves with their united force against the boat trying to push it off. They shoved till they were purple in the face, but the boat refused to budge. They could not stir it a single inch.

Gustav took off his shoes and stockings and got into the water. "Now!" he cried. "All hands, push! Push!" Suddenly he slipped on the slimy, submarine grass and weed and vanished from view for a while.

At last he bobbed up again and spat out a pint of salt water. Then he called the boat several angry names, and, taking off his dripping clothes, hung them up to dry on the palm tree.

"You see," said the Professor. "That palm is of some use to us after all."

They went back to the boat again, and sweated and tugged for half an hour like furniture removers transporting a piano downstairs.

But the sailing-boat was no piano. It remained obstinately fixed where it was.

"The beast!" muttered Hans Schmauch. "Come on, chaps. Push! Push!"

In vain. Love's labour lost. They sat down wearily in the sand to recover their breath. "A nice outlook!" said Gustav. "What on earth are we going to do if we can't get our ship afloat?"

Schmauch lay down on his back and closed his eyes. "We'll haul down the sail and become a little island race. A good thing we brought some tinned food!"

Gustav got up to see whether his clothes were drying. He wrung them out. "Now there's nothing to hinder our independent development," he said. "Not even a tele-phone or a letter-box. We're jolly old Robin-son Crusoes."

The Professor struck the ground with his fist. "We must get back," he cried. "We *must*! Or Mr. Byron will give us all the slip."

Gustav looked round. There was nothing but sea and clouds. He laughed wryly. "We shall have to walk back, Professor."

Chapter 11

PASSPORT INSPECTION

Evening was coming on. Dusk would soon be falling. The sun sank behind a cloud, and clouds and sea were inundated with floods of rosy light.

Emil and Little Tuesday had been standing for over an hour on the Korlsbüttel landing-stage, waiting impatiently for their friends' return. Emil had cut them some sandwiches. Tuesday was holding the packet. He was in the highest spirits, and looking forward to what was about to happen like a king to his coronation.

PASSPORT INSPECTION

Sailing-boats of all sizes came gliding into the harbour, but there was no sign of the boat for which they were waiting.

"There they are!" shouted Tuesday, and pointed to a little yacht that was nearing the landing-stage.

But it was not they.

"I can't understand it," said Emil. "I hope they haven't had an accident."

"I don't see how they could; there hasn't been a storm or anything. I expect they sailed out too far and it's taking them longer to get back than they expected."

"Have you seen anything of *Kunigunde IV*?" called Emil to the occupants of a returning boat.

"We haven't seen any girls at all," cried the man at the helm, and his friends in the boat laughed heartily.

"What an ass!" said Tuesday.

"We'll wait another half hour," Emil decided. "If they haven't got here by then it will be no good waiting for Gustav's motor-bike; we shall have to *walk* to Graal."

They waited.

Then Emil took a sheet of paper from his pocket. "We've gone to Graal without you," he wrote on it. "Please hurry up and be in Heidekrug and Warnemünde as agreed. Password Emil!"

"Half a mo!" he said, and ran down to the harbour. He stuck up the note at the place where *Kunigunde IV* was generally moored and in such a position that it could not be overlooked. He fixed it to a mooring-post with a pin. (He had always carried pins about with him since his experience with Herr Grundeis.)

Then he ran back to Little Tuesday. "No sign of them, I suppose?"

Tuesday shook his head.

"Unreliable blighters!" grumbled Emil. "Well, it's no good hanging about here. We shall have to step out."

PASSPORT INSPECTION

And so they set off for Graal. Sometimes they ran, sometimes they walked. Tuesday carried the sandwiches.

The air was warm and close in the woods. There was a marsh near by. The gnats almost devoured the two hasty pedestrians. Frogs hopped across the path and a cuckoo called from the distance.

After about an hour they came to a meadow on which black and white cows were grazing. One of the cows, or perhaps it was an ox, came galloping at them with lowered horns. They ran for their lives. At last they came to a fence, climbed over, and found themselves on a sandy path that led to the shore. The cow, or ox, glared at them for a moment, turned round and trotted back to the herd.

"The beast!" panted Little Tuesday. "I'm pretty well done up. And I nearly dropped the sandwiches."

"That's Graal over there!" cried Emil.

"And look, there's the steamer from Müritz coming in! We must get a move on!"

About this time, on an island in the midst of the Baltic Sea, the Professor was just looking at his watch. "The steamer's just leaving Graal," he said. "It's enough to drive you mad."

Hans Schmauch, who was sitting by the palm tree, had tears in his eyes. "It's all my fault," he lamented. "Can you chaps forgive me?"

"Don't talk such rot!" said Gustav. "A man's at his best when he's up against it; and Emil will manage this Pachulke chap without our help. Emil and Tuesday know how to look after themselves."

"They can't do it without us. What can Emil and Tuesday do alone? Besides, they'll still be waiting for us at Korlsbüttel. I expect they're just going to the harbour police to tell them our boat's failed to return."

PASSPORT INSPECTION

Gustav disagreed with him. "Why should Emil call in the police? I don't see what can happen to us here. We can sleep in the cabin and we've got plenty of food. And some time tomorrow a fishing-boat or a steamer will come past and we can hail it."

"You're talking through your hat," returned the Professor. "How is Emil to know that we've got stuck on this island? He's not a thought-reader."

This was too much for Gustav. "That's true. I'm sorry. Sometimes I'm a bigger fool than I've any right to be."

"Emil will think we've been shipwrecked," said the piccolo, disconsolately. "He'll think we're clinging to the keel and liable to be drowned at any minute." He blew his nose. "And my uncle will be back from Sweden tomorrow morning."

"I expect he'll give you a licking," said Gustav thoughtfully. "Perhaps we ought to stay on this island for the rest of our lives.

We could live by catching fish, couldn't we? And we could make a tent out of the sail. And perhaps there's some flint on this bally island. Then we could collect driftwood, dry it, make a fire of it and cook the fish. For breakfast, dinner and supper. What do you say?"

"It's the sort of proposal I should expect you to make," said the Professor ironically. "Perhaps some day coconut palms will grow here. Then we could cook gulls' eggs in the shells, and put the milk in our breakfast coffee."

"But have we got any coffee?" asked Gustav.

"No, but you've got a screw loose," replied the Professor. "Hans, how long will the drinking-water last?"

"About a day if we're sparing with it," answered the piccolo.

"We shall have to be more sparing that that," said the Professor firmly. "It will have to last two days. I hope it rains in the morning. Then we can put out some empty tins and collect the rain-water."

"Great!" cried Gustav. "Professor, you're still the old master-mind."

"I'm going to lock up the provisions," said the Professor. "And hand them out myself."

Gustav put his hands over his ears. "Don't keep talking about food," he said. "You'll make me hungry."

The Professor went to the water's edge and looked across the sea.

Gustav poked Hans Schmauch in the ribs. "Do you know who he looks like?"

"No."

"Napoleon on St. Helena," whispered Gustav, and chuckled.

When the steamer put in at Korlsbüttel, Emil and Tuesday watched carefully through the cabin-window. Tuesday flattened his nose against the glass. "But suppose Byron doesn't come aboard?"

"Then we'll dash up and jump ashore just before they cast off," returned Emil. "But look! Here he comes!"

Mr. Byron and Mackie, the smaller twin, came up the gangway. They brought with them five large trunks. At last they were all stowed away, and Byron went and looked over the rail, while Mackie sat down on a seat. The official on the landing-stage unslung the rope and threw it to one of the sailors. The motor began to throb, and the ship moved slowly off.

The two boys watched the shore as the lighted windows of Korlsbüttel grew smaller and smaller. The water began to splash against the portholes.

"There's such a smell of oil," whispered Tuesday. "I hope I'm not going to be sick."

Emil opened the porthole. The cold night air streamed in and salt water splashed into their faces. Tuesday put out his head and drew in a deep breath. Then he sat down on

214

a seat and smiled at Emil. "What would my parents say if they knew?" he remarked.

Emil thought for a moment of his mother in Neustadt and his grandmother in Copenhagen. Then he pulled himself together and patted Tuesday's knee. "It will all come right," he said. "You see Hans Schmauch will come aboard at Heidekrug and then we shall know that the others are at their posts. The rest is easy."

Emil was mistaken. Hans Schmauch did not come aboard at Heidekrug.

This was certainly a bit of a shock for Emil and Tuesday, but it was a much greater one for Mr. Byron. He sat down beside little Mackie and scratched his head. Away on the shore they could see the moors of Rostock gliding past.

Emil got up. Tuesday moved nervously on his seat. "What is it?" he asked in a low voice.

"We can't wait any longer," said Emil. "The others haven't turned up, so we shall have to tackle the matter ourselves. Come on!" They climbed up the steps and looked round the deck for the Byrons.

A man and a boy were sitting, surrounded by trunks, behind the funnel.

Emil went up to them, while Tuesday kept close behind him, still carrying the packet of sandwiches they had cut for their friends.

"I want to speak to you, Mr. Byron," said Emil.

"What's wrong?" inquired the man, looking up in surprise.

"My friends have sent me here," said Emil. "We know that you expected Hans Schmauch to come aboard at Heidekrug, and that you were going to take him away with you."

An angry light came into Byron's eyes. "So that's why he didn't come, is it? You little brats persuaded him not to turn up?"

"Try to talk decently. I haven't called you by the name you deserve."

PASSPORT INSPECTION

"I wish you would," said Tuesday.

"There's somebody with you, is there?" exclaimed Byron.

"Good evening, Herr Pachulke," said Little Tuesday.

The man laughed savagely.

"We've come here on account of Jackie," said Emil. "Aren't you ashamed of yourself for deserting the poor boy like this?"

"He's no use to me any longer."

Tuesday stepped forward firmly. "And why not? Because he's getting too heavy. We know! But is that any reason to desert him?"

"Of course it is," returned the acrobat. "I couldn't go on working with him. He was spoiling my act. I'm an artiste, if you know what that means. I could get bookings at the London Coliseum! If I'd known two years ago that he was going to grow like this . . . Oh, I could kick myself."

Emil began to lose his temper. "Do it then. We're not going to stop you. I don't know how a man can be such a brute. What's to become of Jackie?"

"Is he to go begging?" asked Tuesday. "Or to drown himself in the sea, or go into an orphanage? We won't stand for it."

"My friends and I," announced Emil, "have decided unanimously that you must come back with us to Korlsbüttel."

"Oh, indeed!" Mr. Byron rolled his eyes. "You'd better keep your noses in your school-books, you young fools!"

"But it's holidays now, Herr Pachulke," answered Tuesday.

"On no account," cried Emil, "will we let you ruin the life of one of the twins simply because he's growing and putting on weight. You've got to come back with us. In a few minutes we shall be in Warnemünde. Our friends will be waiting for us there. And if you refuse to come ashore we shall call the police."

218

PASSPORT INSPECTION

The allusion to the police appeared to disconcert Mr. Byron.

"Well?" asked Emil after a moment's silence. "Are you going to do your duty as a father, or shall we have you arrested?"

The man's face suddenly assumed an expression of relief. "My duty as a father?" he repeated.

"Yes, Herr Pachulke," cried Tuesday, indignantly. "I suppose such an idea has never entered your head."

Mr. Byron smiled grimly. "So that's why this little idiot keeps calling me Pachulke, is it? My name's not Pachulke!"

The two boys looked at him in surprise. "What is it, then?"

"Anders," he answered.

"Have you any papers to prove it?" asked Tuesday.

"My passport," said Herr Anders.

"May I see your passport?" Tuesday asked politely, and when the artiste hesitated, he

219

added: "You can show it to the police if you'd rather."

The man took his passport from his pocket. Tuesday studied it calmly, like a customs officer at a frontier station.

"Is the description accurate?" inquired Emil.

"The name's all right," said Tuesday. "Mr. Byron's real name is Anders." Then he read aloud: "Profession – variety artist. Figure – exceptionally tall and strong. Face – broad. Colour of hair – black. Special features – tatooed on right arm." He handed back the passport to its owner. "Thank you."

Emil felt as if the deck of the ship had vanished from under his feet. "So you're not Jackie's father at all?"

"No," growled Herr Anders. "Neither his father nor his mother. Jackie and Mackie are not twins at all, they are not even related to each other. And Mackie's not my son either. His real name is . . ."

PASSPORT INSPECTION

"Joseph Kortejohann," volunteered Mackie. "The name Byron and all that stuff about being twins is part of the business. Of course I'm sorry for Jackie. Anybody would be. But the fact of the matter is we can't work with him any more. He's growing too fast. He's unlucky."

The shaft of light from Warnemünde lighthouse was sweeping across sea and sky, and the bright windows of the hotels were twinkling a friendly welcome.

Emil had not yet recovered from the shock he had received, but he pulled himself together. "All the same I think it unfair to desert Jackie like that. I feel responsible for him and so do my friends. You'll have to hand over some money to help him till he can find something to do."

"What do you take me for?" cried Herr Anders indignantly. "I'm not going to give money to little urchins I've never seen in my life."

Emil took a piece of paper from his pocket. "We shall give you a receipt with both our signatures."

"And what if I refuse?" asked the man, sarcastically.

"I shouldn't if I were you," said Emil. "If you refuse we shall hand you over to the police."

"But I'm not Jackie's father," Herr Anders shouted. "What can the police do to me?"

"They'll soon tell you that," said Tuesday, gently. "They know their own job."

Emil sat down under a lamp. "I'm writing out a receipt for one hundred marks."

"Have you gone mad?" stormed the man. He had suddenly turned very pale. "A hundred marks! You want your necks wringing."

"That's too much," intervened Mackie. "By the time we've bought our tickets we should have nothing left."

"Is that true?" asked Tuesday.

PASSPORT INSPECTION

"Yes," said Mackie. "Word of honour."

"All right, fifty marks," agreed Emil. He wrote out the receipt and signed it. "Come on, Tuesday, sign here."

Tuesday wrote his name on the receipt and Emil held it out to Herr Anders. But Herr Anders did not produce the money.

By this time the steamer was nearing the landing-stage.

"As you like," said Emil sternly.

The boat stopped and was made fast.

"I'm going for the captain," said Emil. He went towards the bridge and was on the point of ascending the stairs, when Herr Anders called on him to stop, snatched a wallet from his pocket and held out a banknote.

Emil took the note. It was for fifty marks. "Thank you," he said. "Here's the receipt."

Herr Anders began to pick up his luggage. "Keep it," he growled, "and go to the devil!" Then he strode off down the gangway.

Mackie had followed him a few steps when he looked back.

"Remember me to Jackie!" he shouted. Then he trotted after the giant Anders and disappeared. Emil put the receipt in his trouser-pocket.

Shortly afterwards he and Tuesday were in the station, studying time-tables. Emil shrugged his shoulders. "The last train's gone, old man, and so has the last boat. But we must get back to Korlsbüttel somehow and find out what's happened to the others. I hope they've got back all right."

"We shall have to walk then," said Little Tuesday.

Emil nodded. "I think we can do it in three hours."

"All right. Come on," rejoined Tuesday in a tired voice. "The night-march through the desert! I feel like a soldier in the Foreign Legion."

"I've given up feeling at all," said Emil.

224

PASSPORT INSPECTION

While Gustav, the Professor and Hans Schmauch were asleep in the stranded sailing-boat; while Captain Schmauch was drinking hot punch in the cabin of his steamer as it ploughed its way across the Baltic, and while Emil and Tuesday were trudging down the dark road that led to Markgrafenheide, our visitors to Copenhagen were sitting at a tasty dinner in their hotel across the road from the Opera House. The coach-ride through Zealand, the inspection of Hamlet's tomb and of the castle of Helsingborg had given them keen appetites. They ate heartily and they laughed and talked.

But Frau Haberland, the Professor's mother, was more silent than usual and her smile came more rarely.

"What is it, dear?" asked Herr Haberland. "A headache?"

"I don't know what it is, but somehow I'm afraid. I have a feeling that something has gone wrong with the boys at Korlsbüttel."

Herr Haberland put his arm round his wife's shoulder. "But, my dear, you mustn't give way to these fixed ideas. Whenever we leave Theodore, you think a roof-tile's going to fall on his head." He laughed. "The boys are keen on independent development. We must give them a chance, or they'll be getting restive. Now, darling, cheer up."

She smiled, but only to do him a favour. She did not believe him.

An hour later a milk-van overtook two boys trudging slowly down the road to Heidekrug.

The driver pulled up his horse. "Where do you want to get to?"

"Korlsbüttel," answered the taller of the two. "Can you give us a lift?"

"Jump up behind," said the driver. "But don't go to sleep or you'll fall into the road."

Emil helped Tuesday on to the van and climbed up beside him. The man drove on. In one minute Little Tuesday was asleep.

PASSPORT INSPECTION

Emil held him in his arms and, while Tuesday slept, looked across at the dark woods or upward at the starry sky. He was thinking of all that had happened during the day. "Have I made a mess of things? What's to become of Jackie now? And where are Gustav and the Professor?"

An owl flew silently over the tree-tops. The horse shied. The driver called to it gruffly.

In his sleep Tuesday threw both arms – one hand still holding the packet of sandwiches – round Emil's neck. "Password Emil!" he muttered.

Chapter 12

THE CAPTAIN'S RETURN

Early on Wednesday morning Captain Schmauch landed in Korlsbüttel. The stevedores were waiting on the quay to unload the cargo. When the captain had completed the usual formalities with the customs officers, he went ashore. Feeling chilly, he walked up to the Strand Hotel to get a cup of hot coffee.

Scarcely had the waiter taken his order, when the manager came hurrying up, wished the captain good morning and asked him whether he had any idea of where his nephew was.

THE CAPTAIN'S RETURN

The captain laughed heartily. "You will have your little joke, won't you? Send the lad here. I want a word with him."

"But he's not in the hotel! He had his day off yesterday and since then he's never been back. And last night Mr. Byron and one of his twins suddenly vanished. What a life!"

The captain sprang to his feet. "Never mind that coffee!" he cried. And he ran as fast as his old seaman's legs would carry him down to the harbour. His sailing-boat was not there. His knees gave; he looked round for assistance and caught sight of a note pinned to one of the mooring-posts.

He knelt down, tore it off and read it. It was Emil's note of the previous evening.

The captain rose with an effort and ran panting into the village. At last he reached "Seaside Villa". He threw open the garden gate and grabbed the front-door handle. The door was locked. He ran round the house and peered through the glass of the veranda.

Emil Tischbein was sitting on a chair with his arms and head lying on the table. He was fast asleep.

Little Tuesday was lying on the sofa by the wall. He was wrapped in a camel-hair rug and only a lock of his hair could be seen above the sofa-cushion. He, too, was sleeping soundly.

The veranda door was locked. Captain Schmauch drummed on the pane with his fists, first softly; then, when the boys did not wake, harder and harder.

At last Emil looked up, very sleepily. Suddenly a look of recognition came into his eyes. He glanced round the veranda, passed the fingers of one hand through his tousled hair, jumped to his feet and unlocked the door.

"Where's Hans?" asked the captain.

Emil quickly told him all he knew. "We didn't get back from Warnemünde till after midnight," he concluded. "Tuesday never woke up at all. I lifted him off the van, lugged him on to this sofa and covered him up. I sat down on the chair to wait for morning. I'd made up my mind to inform the harbour police and to break the news to Jackie and give him the fifty marks as some kind of compensation. And if your boat weren't found I was going to telegraph to the Hotel d'Angleterre, Copenhagen." He shrugged his shoulders. "But I must have fallen asleep. I'm very sorry, captain. What are you going to do now?"

Old Captain Schmauch went to the door. "I'm going to get all the motor-boats I can to search the sea. Wake your friend and come down to the harbour." He ran off as quickly as he could.

Emil went to the sofa and shook Tuesday till he woke. They hastily cleaned their teeth, washed, opened the packet of sandwiches, which Tuesday had carried about with him all the day before, and ran out of the house eating them.

Emil stopped at the crossroads. "Tuesday, run down to the harbour. Perhaps you can help the captain. I shall wake Jackie and bring him with me." He ran towards the dunes.

"Ahoy!" shouted Tuesday, and made off towards the harbour.

Half an hour later twenty-two fishing-smacks, three yachts and seven motor-boats put out from Korlsbüttel harbour. Beyond the harbour-mouth they spread out fanwise. It was arranged that they should keep in sight of each other, and in this way it was hoped that nothing at all conspicuous would be overlooked.

Captain Schmauch stood at the helm of the motor-boat *Argus*, which its owner, the proprietor of a factory, had placed at his disposal. Emil, Tuesday and Jackie were kneeling on the seats, looking attentively across the sea. Sometimes the boat heeled over till the salt water spurted into the boys' faces.

"I don't believe I've thanked you," said Jackie. "It was such a shock. The first shock's always the best. Well, thank you very much! And especially for the money!" He shook hands with them. "Well, now I must give an eye to poor old Uncle Schmauch. He's feeling a good deal worse than I am. You know there's not much harm can happen to me. I've got the thickest skin in Central Europe."

He went up to the captain and nodded to him cheerfully. "Don't let this get you down, skipper!" he said. "I'm sure it's nothing very serious. I can feel it. You see, I've got the fourth dimension."

The captain looked straight ahead and smiled grimly.

Jackie looked round. Away to his left a dark fishing-boat was cutting through the waves, and far to his right, a snow-white yacht. "By the way, skipper, are there any sandbanks

233

about here, or little islands or anything of that sort?"

The old sailor let go of the wheel for a moment and the boat spun over the waves like a top. Then he resumed his grip more firmly than ever. "Heavens!" he cried excitedly. "That's an idea. I hope you're right."

He said no more. But he changed his course.

The three Robinson Crusoes had awakened very, very early. Shivering as though they had slept in an ice-house, they had crawled out of the cabin and performed violent physical exercises till the sun rose higher.

Then they had taken a few sips of water and breakfasted on tinned provisions. Now the empty tins were standing open-mouthed in the sand waiting for rain. But there was no rain. On the contrary, the sky was bluer than it had been for days.

"I should never have believed," said

THE CAPTAIN'S RETURN

Twenty-two fishing-smacks, three yachts and seven motor-boats
put out from Korlsbüttel

Gustav, "that you could get so angry at fine weather. Well, you're always learning."

"If we had no tins," said the Professor petulantly, "it would rain in torrents. That's how it always is."

"Still, everything has its compensations," returned Gustav. "Suppose you had written your essay the other day about the most interesting experience of your holiday – you'd simply have to throw it in the fire."

"It seems to me doubtful whether we shall ever write essays again," said the Professor dejectedly.

"If that's all there was to it, I shouldn't much mind," cried Gustav. "But the thought of never seeing my motor-bike again is pretty grim." He whistled softly to himself.

Hans Schmauch took off his white shirt and hoisted it in place of a flag. "That may help them to find us," he remarked.

Later on they made another attempt to get

the *Kunigunde* afloat. She swayed but refused to budge.

"The beastly thing's taken root during the night," said Hans Schmauch. "It's no good . . . Listen to me," he went on, when they were sitting in the sand again, "all this is my fault. The drinking-water will only last till tomorrow morning. If somebody doesn't find us by this afternoon, I shall put on one of the life-belts from the locker and try to swim to the mainland. I shall probably meet a fishing-boat or a steamer on the way."

"Don't talk rot!" exclaimed Gustav. "If there's any swimming to be done I'm the one to do it."

"It's my fault," insisted the piccolo, "so I've got to take the consequences."

"I don't know what you're talking about," returned Gustav. "The best swimmer is obviously the man to swim ashore."

"Just what I think," said Hans Schmauch. "Well then?"

"But I'm the best swimmer."

"No, I am!"

They sprang to their feet. They were about to close with each other when the Professor threw a handful of sand into their faces. They spat vigorously and wiped the sand from their eyes. "You must be absolutely mad," said the Professor, calmly. "Why don't you lie down and sleep for a few hours. Then you'd forget about eating and drinking and the supplies would last longer."

They lay down obediently in the sand and closed their eyes.

The Professor sat down in the boat, leaned against the mast and kept watch over the horizon.

The motor-boat *Argus* ploughed its way resolutely through the waves. Sometimes, when the boys forgot to hold tight, they toppled off the seat and slid across to the farther side of the boat. Tuesday had a large bump on his forehead. Captain Schmauch stood at the helm like a statue gazing across the waste of waters. They looked the way he was looking. "There!" he cried suddenly and pointed into the distance. But they could see nothing.

"A white flag!" he cried excitedly. "There they are." He nodded to Jackie. "That question of yours was worth its weight in gold, my boy."

"What question, skipper?"

"Whether there were any islands about here. The boys have run aground on the island with the palm tree planted on it. I'll give them what-for when I get my hands on them."

The boys crowded round him. "I knew at once that nothing serious had happened," said Jackie.

The captain laughed with relief. "That's right. Of course you've got the fourth dimension."

"Now I can see something white! And a mast!" cried Emil.

"So can I!" shouted Jackie.

Tuesday could not see anything yet. When Emil tried to show him which way to look, he found that the little boy was crying. The tears were coursing down his sunburnt cheeks.

"What's the matter, Tuesday?"

"I'm so awfully glad," stammered Tuesday. "But you needn't tell Gustav and the Professor that I blubbed on their account. Or they'll be getting so cocky, the silly idiots." He laughed through his tears.

Emil promised to keep his secret.

"I can see all three of them!" cried the captain. "And that's my *Kunigunde*. All right, my lads, you wait till I get my hands on you!"

Gustav and the piccolo were leaping about the tiny island like hottentots, yelling and waving their arms.

The Professor was sitting quite still, writing with his finger in the sand. Presently he got up, collected the empty tins and threw them one by one into the sea.

Hans Schmauch climbed into the boat, hauled down his shirt, and quickly put it on.

Then the motor-boat came shooting through the spray. The engine stopped. The captain threw a rope, which Hans Schmauch adroitly caught and knotted firmly to the stern of the sailing-boat. Now the two vessels were lying close together.

"Hurrah, you loobies!" shouted Gustav.

Captain Schmauch was the first on board the *Kunigunde IV.*

His nephew went up to him. "It's all my fault, Uncle," he said.

The captain gave him a box across the ears that could have been heard a long way off. "Thank goodness you're all safe and sound!" he cried.

Chapter 13

THE NEXT STEPS

The return of the large fleet of rescue boats and the arrival of the shipwrecked youngsters developed into quite a festival. Natives and visitors were wedged in a thick crowd on the landing-stage and the quay, and even filled the neighbouring streets. They waved their hands. It was about lunch-time and the midday meal was scorching in over twenty kitchens.

Captain Schmauch sent the boys by a roundabout path to the Strand Hotel. He, himself, accompanied the sailors and fishermen who had helped him in the search. He treated them to two barrels of beer and two rounds of spirits. When he had drunk their health and thanked them heartily he strode off to the Strand Hotel and ordered a good meal for himself and the boys.

For the sake of privacy the meal was laid for them in the club-room, and there they ate like hunters. Meanwhile each party gave a detailed report to the other of what had happened. Although Hans Schmauch was really the hotel piccolo he sat at table with the rest of the party and was waited on in the most amiable manner by his immediate superior, Herr Schmidt, the waiter.

The sweet consisted of chocolate pudding with vanilla sauce.

"I should like to suggest," said the captain, "that we keep quiet about the adventure some of you had on that desert island. To-morrow your old people will be coming back from Denmark. There's no need for them to know a word about it. But if you find you can't keep it to yourselves you must put all the blame on me. I'll fix it up somehow."

Emil and the Professor jumped to their feet.

The captain waved his hand. "I know what you're going to say. Of course you've got your pride and want to take the blame for your own mistakes." He shook his head. "It's bad enough for you to have given me a shock. Spare the others. We old folk are very nervous."

Emil and the Professor sat down again.

"So that's that!" said the captain kindly. "And now Uncle Schmauch is going to sell his timber." He turned his head and called for the bill.

When the boys left the table they ran down to the harbour. All except Hans Schmauch, who put on his black suit and became a piccolo again as though nothing had happened. The others fetched from the *Kunigunde IV* the market-basket with what was left of the provisions, carried it solemnly back to the house and put it in the pantry. Gustav suddenly became self-important. "I'm on duty today," he cried. "And about time!" Then he spread out the stock-list on the kitchen-table and made up his accounts as well as he could.

They sent Jackie Pachulke to the hotel to fetch his trunk and the rest of his belongings. While he was away they set up in their bedroom the camp-bed, of which Klotilde had once told them. Jackie could not stay any longer at the hotel.

"We ought really to have a good long sleep now," said the Professor, when that job was done. He had caught cold on the island, despite the tropical palm, and talked thickly through his nose. "But we've no time for sleeping just yet; we've got to make up our minds what we're going to do for Jackie. It's a good thing Herr Anders coughed up the fifty marks, but Jackie can't live on that. He's got no parents or brothers and sisters. Goodness only knows when he'll get another job. Any suggestions?"

Little Tuesday put up his hand. "Let's go into the garden. Then we four detectives can each go into a different corner and try to think of something. In five minutes we can all meet at the garden table and report what we've thought of."

The proposal was accepted. They ran out into the garden, each to a different corner, and set themselves to think.

The weather was alarmingly fine. Crickets were twanging their mandolins, grasshoppers springing from grass blade to grass blade, and from the alder-coppice came the piping of an oriole.

Five minutes later the boys met, as agreed, at the large, round garden table and took their seats as gravely as a bench of magistrates.

THE NEXT STEPS

Emil looked round. "It looks to me as if somebody's missing," he said.

"Gustav!" cried Tuesday.

They ran to Gustav's corner. The champion motor-cyclist was lying full-length in the grass, fast asleep.

The Professor shook him vigorously. "Hey!"

Gustav slowly opened his eyes. "What's up?"

"You were sent here to think," said Little Tuesday, reproachfully.

Gustav sat up. "All right. How am I to think if you come here shouting at me?"

"Oh, so you have been thinking?" said Emil. "Tell us what you've thought of."

"Nothing, you looby."

They laughed. Then they dragged him to his feet and all trotted back to the table.

"The meeting is open," declared the Professor. "Emil will speak first."

Emil rose. "Hearers and fellow-detectives!

EMIL AND THE THREE TWINS

On Friday next, the day after tomorrow, the film of *Emil and the Detectives* is to be shown in Korlsbüttel at the Lighthouse Cinema. We had decided not to let people know who we are, but simply to go to the film like other members of the public. But now I've come to the conclusion that we can help Jackie by revealing our secret and telling the owner of the cinema who we are. If we do he can issue a leaflet, or paste a strip over the posters, saying that Emil and the Detectives will be present in person at such and such performances. Perhaps that will bring more children to his cinema, and he will be able to help Jackie by giving him the takings of the first performance. He will profit by taking more money throughout the run." Emil sat down.

The others beamed all over their faces.

"Any objections?" asked the Professor. "I should think not. The proposal is first-rate." He paused. "Emil's proposal is carried unanimously. And now I have something to say. I suggest that one of us should go to the offices of the local paper and speak to the editor. He must write an article, or get one of us to write it, describing how Jackie was deserted by this Herr Anders. It must be published at once and it must state that all the children in Korlsbüttel and the other places along the coast should make a collection for Jackie Byron. The money ought to be paid into the newspaper's bank account and the amount of the collection announced in a few days by the editor." He sat down.

"Great!" cried Gustav. "Any objections? No. The Professor's proposal is carried unanimously. Tuesday!"

Little Tuesday got up. "I wanted to propose that Gustav and perhaps somebody else goes round on his motor-bike to all the towns along the coast and tells the children on the beach exactly what's happened and why Jackie needs help. Perhaps we could put up notices and sign them: 'Emil and the Detectives'. But that comes to much the same as Emil's idea." He sat down.

"Bravo!" cried the others.

"If I'd thought of anything," said Gustav, "we should have had so many ideas we shouldn't have known what to do with them."

For some time they discussed the pros and cons. Then they ran on to the veranda and wrote out eight posters, one for Korlsbüttel, one for Graal, one for Müritz, one for Heide-krug, one for Warnemünde, one for Heiligen-damm, one for Ahrenshoop and one for Brunshaupten.

Then Gustav fetched his motor-cycle from the pavilion and pushed it into the road. Tuesday perched himself on the carrier with the eight posters under his arm and off they went. Emil and the Professor waved to them as they vanished round the corner.

When Jackie came back with his luggage they asked him to look after the house. Leaving him behind, they ran off to the village.

But they did not tell him why they were in such a hurry.

When Emil entered the office of the Lighthouse Cinema, Herr Bartelmann, the owner, said he was much too busy to see him. Five minutes later Herr Bartelmann looked up from his desk and found Emil still standing there. "Haven't you gone?" he asked in surprise. "What is it?"

"I'm Emil Tischbein."

Herr Bartelmann leaned back in his chair. "What about it?"

"I'm the Emil whose adventures have been made into a film, and you're going to show it the day after tomorrow."

"I'm very pleased to meet you," said the owner of the cinema. "Go on!"

Emil explained the detectives' plan to him.

Herr Bartelmann screwed up his eyes. He always did that when he wanted to think. Then he clicked his tongue against the roof

251

of his mouth like a horse-dealer when a new horse is led into the ring. Herr Bartelmann scented a bit of business. "You can have the takings from the first performance for this boy on one condition: you must all promise to make a personal appearance after each performance for a week."

"A week!" cried Emil. "After each performance? That's sheer hard labour."

"You can't get something for nothing," said the cinema-owner.

Emil thought for a moment. "All right," he said. "But if we promise to do that we must have the whole of the first day's takings, that is the receipts of the first three performances."

Herr Bartelmann screwed up his eyes again. "Good businessman, eh?" He nodded. "I agree." Then he typed a contract with a carbon copy on his machine. Both signed the two copies and each kept one.

"So that's settled!" said Bartelmann. "Don't be late on Friday."

Emil went out with the contract in his coat-pocket.

Herr Bartelmann took up his telephone and put through a call to the advertising manager of the local paper. He gave orders for the insertion of a big, new advertisement. Then he telephoned to a bill-posting agency and ordered a red strip to be pasted diagonally across all the cinema posters in Korlsbüttel and neighbourhood. These strips were to bear the words in big letters: "Emil and the Detectives will be present in person at every performance throughout the week".

Meanwhile the Professor was seated in a room at the newspaper offices writing the article he had discussed with the editor and an "appeal to the holiday-children". He described Jackie's precarious position and called upon them all to contribute generously and thus assure the immediate future of the little orphaned acrobat. He signed the appeal: "On behalf of Emil and the Detectives, Theodore Haberland, alias the Professor".

He took his article into the next room and gave it to the editor who slowly read it through. Then he called in a messenger-boy: "Go down to the machine-room," he said. "I want this article set at once and put on the front page. I shall be down myself presently." The messenger hurried out.

The telephone rang. The editor took up the receiver. "Call from Graal?" he said. "Who's speaking? Tuesday? Yes. He's with me now."

He handed the receiver to the Professor. "Any news?" asked the Professor into the telephone. "I see. Very good. Yes, no need to alter the posters. Our appeal will be in the paper tomorrow. Tired? So am I. Password Emil!" He hung up the receiver.

"What posters are those?" asked the editor.

The Professor told him.

"An excellent example of organized benevolence," said the editor approvingly. "By the way, that article you wrote is very good. What are you going to do when you grow up?"

"I don't know," answered the Professor. "As a little boy I wanted to be a builder, but I've given up that idea. What interests me most now is breaking up the elements, the atomic theory and positive and negative electrons. I don't understand it all yet, but I'm sure it's a marvellous thing to go in for. Well, I must get back to my friend." He rose and thanked the editor.

"That's quite all right," said the latter, and ushered him to the door.

Meanwhile Gustav and Tuesday were on the beach at Graal. The motor-cycle and seven posters were leaning against the sea-wall. Gustav was just pinning up the eighth poster to the municipal notice-board.

A few children stopped and looked on.

Gustav pressed his hooter.

The number of children increased. Several grown-ups joined them. All were curious to see the notice.

"We ought to say a few suitable words, oughtn't we?" whispered Tuesday to Gustav. "Let me get on your back."

Gustav bent down and Tuesday climbed on to his shoulders. Then he raised his hand.

There was silence.

"Friends," cried Tuesday. "We have come to ask your help, not for ourselves, of course, but for a boy who is in great trouble. We have explained it on the poster just fixed to that notice-board. You will find some more about it in the newspaper tomorrow. If you can't read, you must get someone to read it to you. We are visiting eight places this afternoon and we hope that you children will not leave us in the lurch. My friends and I are Emil and the Detectives. Perhaps you have already heard of us. The chap I'm sitting on is Gustav with the Hooter."

Gustav bowed and Tuesday nearly pitched head-first into the sand.

"And I," declared the speaker, "I am . . ."

"You must be Tuesday," cried a little girl. "Aren't you?"

"Yes. But it's not all that important, as Gustav says. The main thing is for you to give all you can and make a big collection. And now we must be getting on. Let me get down, Gustav!"

"Half a mo," growled Gustav. "I've got an idea – and that doesn't often happen to me. Listen here, you little beggars," he shouted. "You can put the money you collect in the post-office savings-bank." Then he lifted Tuesday down. And the two detectives with the seven posters climbed on to the motor-cycle.

"We shall see you all on Friday," cried Tuesday.

"At the Lighthouse Cinema! Password Emil!"

"Password Emil!" yelled the children of Graal.

The motor-cycle sped down the forest-path that led into the village. Gustav hooted. The propaganda trip on behalf of Jackie Byron, alias Paul Pachulke, was well launched.

THE NEXT STEPS

"We have come to ask your help," cried Tuesday

Chapter 14

A SERIOUS CONVERSATION

On Thursday the grown-ups arrived back in Korlsbüttel. They had come from the Danish island of Bornholm, and Fräulein Klotilde Seelenbinder was still rather green in the face. She had been seasick on the boat and said she could feel the earth rocking under her feet.

Herr Haberland got some valerian drops from the medicine chest and she had to take them. "It's a disgrace," she said, "to let things get you down so." Then she marched off to the kitchen, compared the boys' stock-list with the contents of the pantry and presently set off for the village, still rather unsteady on her feet, to buy food for the midday meal.

The other travellers had escaped sea-sickness, and talked at great length about Copenhagen, Zealand and Bornholm. Pony Hütchen read a few lines from the rough notes in her diary. In their heart of hearts they were all glad to be home again. "Hotel beds are hotel beds when all's said and done!" observed Emil's grandmother. "I'm going to lie down upstairs till lunch-time just to find out what a real bed feels like again." She went upstairs with Pony. Herr Haberland inquired whether anything serious or disturbing had happened during their absence.

The boys thought of the advice the captain had given them, and shook their heads.

"Just as I expected," said Herr Haberland, and went on to tell them of the apprehensions that had troubled his wife on Tuesday evening. He laughed rather patronizingly.

"Women are such nervous creatures. Your mother was quite upset, Theodore, and thought you boys were in great danger. Another proof of how foolish it is to take any notice of the inner voice which afflicts sensitive women. It's merely the result of melancholic depression."

The detectives looked at each other but prudently kept silent. Tuesday took the opportunity of moving out of "Seaside Villa". He fetched his pyjamas and toothbrush from the next room, thanked them for their hospitality and returned to the boarding-house where his father and mother were awaiting him.

Then the Professor told his father the main facts of their pursuit of Mr. Byron and their plans to set Jackie on his feet again. "Jackie slept here last night in the camp-bed," he said. "He's visiting Hans Schmauch at the moment, but if you have no objection he could stay here till something turns up."

Herr Haberland agreed. "I'm glad you have managed so well and have thought of others besides yourselves. You've spent the time very well."

They thought of their escapade on the island and felt distinctly uncomfortable under all this approval.

Gustav of course had something to say for himself. "All the same, it's not a bad thing sometimes to have grown-ups about."

The boys started. Emil trod hard on Gustav's toes.

Gustav pulled a face.

"What's the matter?" asked Herr Haberland.

"Stomach-ache," explained Gustav. It was the only thing he could think of.

Herr Haberland got up at once and went to fetch the valerian drops. Gustav was bursting with health, but there was nothing for it but to swallow the medicine.

The boys grinned like Cheshire cats at his discomfiture.

"If you don't feel better in ten minutes," said Herr Haberland, "you must have another spoonful."

"Lord preserve us!" cried Gustav quickly. "I'm quite well already!"

"I'm glad to hear it," said Herr Haberland delightedly. "There's nothing to compare with valerian drops."

The captain looked in after lunch. They were still sitting at table. He paid his respects to the travellers and took from his pocket a copy of the local paper. "You boys do things on the grand scale," he said. "You've mobilized the whole coast for this Jackie. And, by the way, where is he?"

"With Hans Schmauch," answered Emil. "With your nephew."

The captain handed the paper to the grown-ups. The boys looked over their shoulders and all read the Professor's appeal together. All but the author, who remained sitting on his chair, though he would have given the world to see how this masterpiece looked in print.

Finally the captain pointed out to them the large advertisement of the Lighthouse Cinema, announcing that Emil and the Detectives would appear at every performance for a week, and that the first day's receipts would be handed over to Jackie Byron.

Herr and Frau Haberland, Klotilde Schlips and Pony were enthusiastic, particularly Pony.

But Emil's grandmother asked: "What does this boy, this Jackie, himself say to your charity ramp?"

"Jackie?" repeated Gustav. "He doesn't know anything about it yet."

"I thought as much," said the old lady. "I thought as much. You're fine fellows! You think of everything to the smallest detail, except the most important thing of all. You never think of that, unfortunately."

They sat there looking very uncomfortable. "You can't see what's before your eyes. Surely you don't need to wait till you're my age before you find out what is really important?" She looked sternly at the detectives. "I hope I'm wrong. But which of you would want other people to go round begging for help and collecting money for you without even a by-your-leave?"

The captain took out a large red handkerchief, and wiped his brow. "Bless my soul!" he cried. "Your grandmother's right, Emil. You boys have made fools of yourselves." He rose to his feet. "I'm just going to slip down and see my nephew, and I'll take the opportunity to break the news to that young acrobat. I hope he's got a thick skin. He'll need it." He put on his peaked cap. "Money is an embarrassing invention," he said. "But of course we live in an age of inventions."

When he had gone the others sat still and thoughtful.

"That's just clever talk," said Klotilde.

"Schlips is right," said the Professor. "If you help somebody when he's down and out, you don't expect to be given a diploma, but neither do you expect reproaches."

"And that's all you get," declared Gustav, "for thinking of other people!"

Jackie was not in the hotel. He was on the tennis-courts, and the captain walked down to see him. He found the young acrobat acting as ball-boy. "Ahoy, skipper!" he cried cheerfully, as he saw the captain coming towards him.

"Ahoy!" answered old Captain Schmauch. "Can I speak to you for a minute?"

Jackie threw two balls to one of the players, and picked up three that were lying by the wire-netting. "Sorry, it's quite impossible at the moment, skipper. I've got a job here as you can see. I earn fifty pfennigs an hour. A man must live, mustn't he? Besides I don't like idling about."

"I see," said the captain. "When'll you have finished?"

"In just under an hour, provided I'm not wanted again."

"Then come to me in just under an hour, provided you're not wanted again."

"O.K. skipper!" cried Jackie. "Ahoy!" Then he threw two more balls to the player.

"Ahoy, my lad!" returned the captain, and trudged off homeward.

Meanwhile Emil and Pony had gone with their grandmother for a walk in the wood. It was a beautiful wood. Between the trees grew broom, wild strawberries, bilberries, dewberries, dog violets and wild pansies. The honeysuckle climbed up the tree-trunks to reach the sunshine.

"Have you been writing regularly to your mother?" asked the old lady.

"Of course. And she's written to me every day."

They sat down in the grass. A yellowhammer was swinging on a birch twig, and wagtails were running busily to and fro on the path. "I wrote to your mother, too," said Emil's grandmother. "From Copenhagen." She watched a may-bug spread out its wings on a grass stem and fly away. "How do you like Inspector Jeschke, Emil?"

Emil started and looked up at her. "What do you know about that?"

"Have you any objection to my daughter asking me whether she ought to marry again?"

"But they decided long ago to get married."

"They've decided nothing," declared

his grandmother. "They've decided nothing."

Pony Hütchen came running up. She showed them a large bunch of wild flowers. "I think I should like to go in for gardening," she said.

"Just as you please," said her grandmother. "Go in for gardening then. Last week you wanted to be a hospital nurse. And the week before a dispenser. Carry on, my girl, carry on! There's only one thing I won't allow: I won't let you be a fireman."

"Well, it is hard to find the right profession," said Pony. "If I were rich I should go in for flying."

"If your grandmother had wheels," observed the old lady, "she'd be an omnibus. And now take your flowers to the house and put them in water. Be off with you!"

Pony preferred to stay in the wood.

"Be off with you!" repeated her grandmother. "Emil and I are discussing a very serious matter."

"I love to hear of serious matters," said Pony.

The old lady looked sternly at her granddaughter.

"Exit Ophelia!" said Pony, shrugging her shoulders, and she walked off, swinging her bunch of flowers.

Emil sat still for a while. They could hear Pony singing in the distance. "So nothing has been decided?" he inquired. "Why hasn't it?"

"I don't quite know. But tell me . . . How do you like the inspector?"

"I can't complain," returned Emil. "We're quite good friends. His Christian name is Heinrich. But the main thing is Mother likes him."

"That's true," admitted his grandmother. "But it seems to me that that's just what you resent. Don't contradict! You think if a woman has such a splendid, affectionate son as you, she doesn't need a husband."

"There's some truth in that," said Emil. "But you put it so crudely."

"I must, my boy, I must! If you won't open your mouth, I can't help exaggerating."

"Mother will never know," he said. "But I didn't think it would happen like that. I thought we should live together all our lives. Just us two. But she's fond of him, and that settles it. I shan't let her notice anything."

"Really?" asked his grandmother. "You should look in the glass now and then. If you go in for self-sacrifice you mustn't go about with a face as long as a fiddle. I'm only a short-sighted old woman but I don't need spectacles to see how you look sometimes. Your mother will find it out one of these days, but then it'll be too late."

She rummaged in her handbag and produced a letter and her reading-glasses. "This is her letter to me. I'm going to read you a

The old lady put down the letter

passage from it." She slowly put on her glasses and began to read: "Jeschke is really a very decent, steady, good-hearted man. I don't know anyone else whom I would rather marry if I marry at all. My dear mother, I can confide in you that I would much rather remain alone with Emil. Of course he has no idea of this and I shall never let him know. But what else can I do? Something might happen to me, and what would become of Emil then? Or I might not earn so much, indeed I'm already earning less than I was. A hairdresser has opened a new shop near the market, and the tradesmen's wives have to go to him or his wife wouldn't trade with them. I must think of my boy's future. I shall be a good wife to Jeschke. I've made up my mind to that. He deserves it. But the only person I really love is my darling boy, my Emil."

The old lady put down the letter.

Emil had slung his arms round his knees.

He looked pale. He gritted his teeth, but suddenly he dropped his head on his knees and began to cry.

"All right, my boy!" said his grandmother. "All right, my boy!" Then she sat there in silence, giving him time to weep. "She's the only one you love," she said after a while, "and you're the only one she loves. Each of you has deceived the other out of love, and in spite of your love you have each misjudged the other. It happens like that sometimes."

A jay flew screaming above the tree-tops.

Emil dried his eyes and looked at the old woman. "What am I to do, Granny?"

"One of two things, Emil. When you get home you can ask her not to marry. Then you'll kiss and the thing will be settled."

"Or?"

"Or you can keep silence, but the silence must last till the end of your days, and you must be cheerful in your silence and not go round with a face like a mourner at a funeral.

You alone can decide which course to pursue. I can only tell you this: You're getting older and your mother is getting older. That sounds simpler than it really is. Will you be able in a few years' time to earn enough for both of you? And if so, where will you earn it? In Neustadt? No, my boy. One day you'll have to leave home, and even if you don't have to, you ought to leave home. Then she will stay behind, all alone ... What will happen if in ten or twelve years you get married? A mother and a young wife don't belong under the same roof. I know. I've tried ... once as the wife and once as the mother." The old lady's eyes seemed to be looking back far into the past. "If she marries she will be making a sacrifice for you. But one day that sacrifice will bring her happiness."

She got up. "Choose which you like ... the one or the other. But think it over carefully. I'm going to leave you alone now."

Emil sprang to his feet. "I'm coming with

you, Granny. I *have* made up my mind. I shall keep silence till the end of my days."

His grandmother looked into his eyes. "Well done!" she said. "Well done! Today you've grown to be a man! . . . There, and now just help me across that ditch."

Chapter 15

THE END OF THE PERFORMANCE

On Friday morning the detectives made the collection for Jackie in Korlsbüttel as they had announced. Tuesday and the Professor worked the beach and the harbour, Gustav the bathing-pool, Emil the village, and Pony the station.

"It's so exciting," she said. "All along the whole coast, further than you can see, children are going round with lists and lead-pencils collecting money for Jackie. Quick, give me a list and a lead-pencil! I can't stand by doing nothing."

THE END OF THE PERFORMANCE

"Aren't you too grown-up for such work?" asked Gustav sarcastically. "If I were a fine young lady like you I wouldn't lift a finger."

She gave him a majestic look. "I don't quarrel with little boys. It's beneath my dignity."

Gustav rolled up his shirt-sleeves, and Pony ran away screaming.

When the boys came home at midday and sat down on the veranda to count the money, Klotilde came running in. She seemed quite demented. "I'm supposed to do the cooking," she cried. "Do you know how many times the bell's rung this morning? Twenty-three! And every time there was some child at the door asking for Emil and the Detectives and wanting to put some money in the collection."

"But Schlips," said the Professor, "that's just what we wanted!"

"Perhaps it is," she returned, morosely.

"But what about my dinner? The milk boiled over, the vegetables have all gone to a mush, and the mutton's burnt black. I'm a cook, not a clerk in a savings-bank."

"In such a good cause," said Gustav, "I can even eat burnt mutton, Fräulein Selbstbinder."

She mumbled something to herself, took a handful of coins from her apron-pocket and put them on the table. "Here! Three marks and ninety pfennigs. I had no time for book-keeping by double entry." She took a deep sniff through her nose. "Gracious goodness! There's something else burning!" And she rushed off to the kitchen.

(She had taken care to conceal the fact that the three marks ninety included fifty pfennigs of her own money. She was a cook with very high principles.)

The boys unloaded their money from every possible sort of pocket, deposited it on the table and sorted it into heaps of copper, nickel and silver. Then they began to count it. It came to forty-three marks. They added up the lists, and reached the same total. Little Tuesday chuckled and added a twenty-mark note. "From my father," he said. "From Big Tuesday."

The Professor ran into the garden, tracked his father to the greenhouse and came back with a ten-mark note. Then they re-counted their pocket-money, made a final sacrifice, and brought the total up to seventy-five marks.

Their faces shone with enthusiasm.

Tuesday produced a clean handkerchief, piled the coins upon it, and tied the corners firmly.

"Are you going to do conjuring tricks?" asked Emil. "I suppose you'll count three and the seventy-five marks will suddenly vanish?"

"I'm going to take it with me," declared Tuesday.

"Where to?" asked the Professor.

"You just leave it here!" cried Pony.

"Leave him alone," said Gustav. "We've got a scheme on. I thought of it myself."

"Good heavens!" cried Pony. "You don't mean to say you've actually thought of something. I hope you're not feeling ill."

"I'm not," he said, and rolled up his sleeves again. "Come over here. We'll visit you tomorrow in hospital." He took a step towards her, but she ran off to Klotilde in the kitchen.

"The little looby," said Gustav. "Just when you've got a good idea, she comes along trying to be funny."

"I'm jolly glad we weren't born girls," declared Tuesday. Then he took his bag of money and set out for home.

Jackie arrived in time for the midday meal. In spite of Klotilde's complaints the roast mutton was excellent. Emil's grandmother turned the conversation to the collection and asked Jackie what he thought of it.

"Well, I'm not finicky in such things," he said. "I've had to work for my living and I've got over being sensitive. Besides what pleases me most is the proof of the detectives' friendship. The skipper agrees with me. You see this morning I spent three hours picking up tennis-balls. That's a collection too, in a way. With tips it amounted to one mark eighty pfennigs. This afternoon I've got two more hours at the same job. That will be another mark. If you take the trouble to work out what that makes in a month, you'll find I should have enough to pay for a furnished room with full board and perhaps a balcony."

They all laughed.

"Isn't that true?" he went on. "On the tennis-courts yesterday, I was feeling full of beans and did a few somersaults from the hand-stand. The tennis-players seemed absolutely nonplussed, and one was so affected that he gave me an old racket. If the game suits me, I might become a coach later on. Then I should rent a few courts, give lessons, and become some day the champion of Germany. Then I should go to Wimbledon and America and perhaps become world champion, or at any rate runner-up. Well, then I should borrow money and open a factory for rackets and all sorts of tennis kit. And lots of people would buy the things I manufactured because my name would be so well known. Of course I shan't call myself Pachulke. You can't become a world champion with a name like that. But I've already been called Byron and I guess I can find another good name when I need one." He bent over his plate and ate voraciously.

"I've no anxiety about him," declared Emil's grandmother.

"No more have I," said Jackie. "There are plenty of jobs for an acrobat who has grown too quickly."

THE END OF THE PERFORMANCE

That afternoon, two steamers put in to the landing-stage, one after the other. One came from the coastal resorts to the west of Korlsbüttel and the other from the east. Hundreds of children came pouring out of the two steamers and Korlsbüttel was swamped by waves of noise and laughter. The crowd was thickest and noisiest outside the Lighthouse Cinema. (The girl in the booking-office was ill for two days.)

The first performance which was to contain the film of *Emil and the Detectives* was timed to begin at four o'clock. Herr Bartelmann, the owner of the cinema, looked into the crowded auditorium. Outside, queues of children were standing waiting for the second performance. Herr Bartelmann was cut to the heart by the knowledge that the day's receipts were not for him. But it was no good crying over spilt milk. He went into his office, where the detectives were waiting, and gave them careful instructions.

When the minor items had been shown the curtains were drawn in front of the screen. The house-lights went up and the curtains opened again.

Now there were four boys and a girl on the stage! The children in the audience stood on their seats, but at last the applause died down and there was silence.

Emil came forward and said in a loud, clear voice: "I thank you on behalf of my friends, my cousin, and myself for coming here. And we all thank you for collecting the money for Jackie. He is a splendid chap or we should not have asked you to help him. After the show he will thank you personally. And now let us all see the Emil-film together. I hope it's good."

A little boy, who was sitting on his mother's knee, called out in a shrill voice: "Are you Emil?"

The children laughed.

"Yes," replied Emil. "I'm Emil Tischbein from Neustadt."

Pony advanced to his side and curtsied. "I'm Pony Hütchen, Emil's cousin."

Then the Professor stepped forward. "I'm the Professor."

Tuesday bowed politely. "I'm Little Tuesday."

Finally it was Gustav's turn. "I'm Gustav with the Hooter. But now I've got a motor-bike." He paused for a moment. "Now, you loobies," he shouted, "are you all here?"

"Yes!" shouted the children.

Gustav laughed. "And what's the password?"

Then they all yelled so loudly that they were heard as far away as the station: "Password Emil!"

Outside the cinema a horse took fright and bolted.

Then the curtains closed again. The lights

in the house went out and the curtains re-opened.

The four words: *Emil and the Detectives* appeared in big letters on the screen.

When the film had come to an end the audience clapped for some minutes without stopping. Then the lights went up again. A girl who was sitting next to Pony said: "You've altered an awful lot since then."

"I'm not the girl in the film at all," said Pony. "She's only playing my part."

"Oh! And the Emil in the film . . . isn't he the real Emil that's sitting by you?"

"No," answered Pony. "The real Emil is my cousin. I've never seen the Emil in the film before. But be quiet now, there's something else to come."

At that moment Jackie appeared on the stage. "You have been collecting money for a boy," he said, as he stepped forward. "And that boy is me. Thanks very much, all of you.

I think it was splendid of you. Later on, when I'm rich, if any of you are broke just come and see me. And don't forget it."

Then Gustav went on to the stage. "On behalf of my friends, the detectives, and of the other children staying in Korlsbüttel, I have pleasure in handing you the proceeds of the Korlsbüttel collection. It amounts to seventy-five marks." With that he handed Jackie a savings-bank book and the two boys shook hands.

Down in the auditorium, the Professor said to Tuesday: "So that was Gustav's idea."

"D'you think it was a bad one?" asked Tuesday.

"It was great," returned the Professor. "Great!"

"And now the representatives of the other districts can come up," announced Gustav from the stage.

Wild confusion broke out below.

At last seven more boys were standing on

the stage, one from Ahrenshoop, one from Grunshaupten, one from Heiligendamm, one from Warnemünde, one from Heidekrug, one from Graal and one from Müritz. And each presented Jackie with a savings-bank book. Jackie had tears in his eyes, though he was really not a bit sentimental.

Gustav quickly examined the bank-books and, when the seven delegates had climbed down from the stage, he announced: "The total collection amounts to six hundred and sixteen marks. Jackie will also have today's takings from this cinema. I congratulate you, Jackie. You're the owner of a fortune. I hope you won't over-eat yourself and get indigestion."

Gustav vanished into the wings.

"I didn't expect all this!" exclaimed Jackie. "I shall have to find a stockbroker."

He took off his coat. "My old friend Skipper Schmauch advised me to do a few tricks, so that you'll be sure I'm the right one. I'm not used to working on my own, but I'll do the best I can." He threw his coat into the wings and stood on his hands. Then he bent his arms till he was standing on his elbows, rose on his hands again and walked from one side of the stage to the other. The audience clapped wildly.

Jackie came down on his feet again. Then he turned a cartwheel, performed a somersault in the air and followed it up with a back bend. Pushing up with his hands he went into a series of hand springs, first with both hands and then with one till he had crossed the whole stage.

To finish up he did back somersaults in the air, starting slowly and getting faster and faster. His head and legs whirled round and round till he looked like a little revolving wheel.

The children shouted, yelled, and clapped their hands till they were sore. Even the grown-ups were quite carried away.

Then the curtains closed. The children who were waiting for the second performance began to crowd into the auditorium. There was a panting and cracking as though a river had burst its banks.

"I liked that somersault," said his grandmother to Emil. "I shall have to practise it tomorrow."

That evening the two steamers put in to the landing-stage again. The children from the seven neighbouring coastal resorts went streaming on board. Parents and nurses were swept along by the current.

Sirens howled to announce their departure. A few stragglers came shouting and waving their hands and stumbled up the gangway. Then a man released the mooring-ropes. The steamers rocked, the paddles churned the water, the engines throbbed and hundreds of handkerchiefs began to wave.

THE END OF THE PERFORMANCE

(Very few of them were quite clean, but by this time it was getting dark.)

"Password Emil!" yelled the children on the steamer that was heading westward. "Password Emil!" screamed the children on the steamer heading eastward.

And "Password Emil!" shouted the Korlsbüttel children from the landing-stage.

"This is the grandest day of my life," said Klotilde Seelenbinder.

Bright coloured lanterns were lighted on the steamers, as they dropped away, one left, one right.

Emil and the Detectives stood at the end of the landing-stage and looked silently after the ships.

Gustav cleared his throat. Then he put his strong arms round the other three boys, who were standing in front of him. "We're always going to be friends, even when we've got long white beards." The others said nothing but they accepted his statement.

Then Jackie came running up. "You're here, are you?" he cried. "I've been looking for you everywhere. Well, I shall never forget today," he added thoughtfully. "I can't realize that I'm the possessor of all that money."

"What have you done with those eight savings-bank books?" asked Tuesday.

"I gave them to Bartelmann to take care of. He's got a fireproof safe in his office. And, what do you think? . . . He's made me an offer. He's asked me to do a turn in his cinema. I'm going to do it for a week on trial."

"What's he going to pay you?" asked the Professor.

"Five marks a day."

The Detectives were delighted.

"And today's takings, which you managed to get for me, amount to about two hundred and fifty marks. He doesn't know exactly how much, but that's about it." Jackie laughed softly. "I just can't believe it. If it goes on like this, I shall buy myself a house next week with hot-water-lighting."

Away across the sea, two little illuminated boats were growing smaller and smaller. The waves broke on the shore, and the white foam shone in the dusk.

"Hans made me promise faithfully," said Captain Schmauch, "that we'd look in at the hotel again. He's been hard at work all day and has not even had time to see the film."

So they decided to call at the hotel. "After all, it's holidays," said Frau Haberland, as she took her husband's arm.

They walked down the landing-stage, the captain and Jackie in front.

"I should like to make a proposal to you," said Captain Schmauch.

"What is it, skipper?"

"My house is small," said the captain, "but it's still a bit too big for me."

"You'd better rent me a room," suggested Jackie.

"That would suit me all right," said the captain. "How long shall you be staying in Korlsbüttel?"

"Till the tennis-courts are closed. I shall stay here as ball-boy till then. And when the season is over, the coach is going to give me an hour's lesson every day. He won't charge much, perhaps he'll do it for nothing."

"You can come and live at my place if you like," said the captain.

"All right, skipper. What's the rent?"

Captain Schmauch gave Jackie a friendly smack. "Don't make silly jokes. You'll be doing me a favour."

"Fine!" said the boy. "Thank you, skipper. We'll sit on the veranda in the evening and play rummy or high-low-jack."

The captain was as pleased as punch.

"And, by the way, do you need any money?" asked Jackie. "I'm well off now. If

THE END OF THE PERFORMANCE

I saved for another week or two I could put a thousand marks into your business. What's the good of keeping it in the savings-bank?"

"All right," said the captain. "That can be arranged. You'll be my sleeping partner, but on one condition – you must spend every summer with me in Korlsbüttel."

"Splendid!" cried Jackie. "And if I find I've no talent for tennis, I'll enter our firm as a cabin-boy."

"Now you're talking," said Captain Schmauch. "I hope you'll find you have no talent."

They laughed and went up the steps to the hotel.

Emil and his grandmother were the last to follow them. They stopped outside the hotel and looked at the sea. One of the steamers had disappeared, the other was still visible on the horizon, like a glowing nutshell.

"I don't believe Jackie really needed our help," said Emil.

"No good deed is wasted, my boy," answered his grandmother. She began to climb the steps. "And now let's send a picture-postcard to your mother."

"Couldn't we send two?"

"Who's the other one for?"

"Inspector Jeschke," he said.

The old lady kissed him.

Red Fox Classics

EMIL
and the
DETECTIVES

ERICH KÄSTNER

'As a matter of fact,' said Emil, 'I'm keeping my eye on a thief.'
'What!' exclaimed the boy with the motor-horn. 'A thief? What has he stolen? Who from?'
'Me,' said Emil, feeling quite important again.

If Mrs Tischbein had known the amazing adventures her son Emil would have in Berlin, she'd never have let him go. Unfortunately, when his seven pounds goes missing on the train journey, Emil is determined to get it back...no mattter what trouble he may run into!

'This book is one of my favourites'
QUENTIN BLAKE
'This must be one of the most delicious children's books ever written'
DAILY EXPRESS

ISBN 0099413124 £4.99

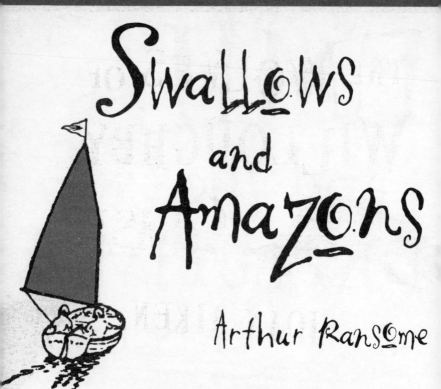

Swallows and Amazons

Arthur Ransome

Titty drew a long breath that nearly choked her.
'It is…' she said.
The flag blowing in the wind at the masthead of the little boat was
black and on it in white were a skull and two crossed bones.
The four on the island stared at each other.

To John, Susan, Titty and Roger, being allowed to use the boat *Swallow* to go camping on the island is adventure enough. But they soon find themselves under attack from the fierce Amazon Pirates, Nancy and Peggy. And so begins a summer of battles, alliances, exploration and discovery.

By the winning author of the first Carnegie medal.

ISBN 0099503913 £4.99

Red Fox Classics

THE WOLVES OF WILLOUGHBY CHASE

JOAN AIKEN

She woke suddenly to find that the train had stopped with a jerk.
'Oh! What is it? Where are we?' she exclaimed before she could stop herself.
'No need to alarm yourself, miss,' said her companion. 'Wolves on the line,
most likely – they often have trouble of that kind hereabouts.'
'Wolves!' Sylvia stared at him in terror.

After braving a treacherous journey through snow-covered wastes
populated by packs of wild and hungry wolves, Sylvia joins her cousin
Bonnie in the warmth and safety of Willoughby Chase. But with
Bonnie's parents overseas and the evil Miss Slighcarp left in charge, the
cousins soon find their human predators even harder to escape.

'Joan Aiken is such a spellbinder that it all rings true…'
THE STANDARD

ISBN 0099411865 £4.99

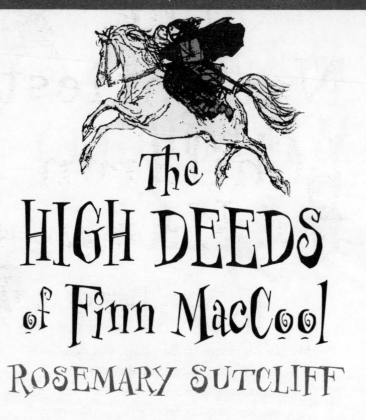

The
HIGH DEEDS
of Finn MacCool
ROSEMARY SUTCLIFF

Then the giant sprang up and seized his club and aimed three mighty blows at Dearmid, which he only just managed to turn on his upflung shield. But he knew that Sharvan expected him to attack with his sword, and so he flung it aside, and the shield with it, and leaping in beneath the giant's guard, twisted his arms about the huge body, and heaving with all his might, flung him over his shoulder and crashing to the ground.

Set in the times of enchanted beasts, fairies and strange creatures, discover the traditional irish legends of Finn MacCool and the Fianna.

ISBN 0099414228   £4.99

The Naughtiest Children I Know

Edited by Anne Harvey

My son Augustus, in the street, one day,
Was feeling quite exceptionally merry.
A stranger asked him: 'Can you show me, pray,
The quickest way to Brompton Cemetery?'
'The quickest way? You bet I can!' said Gus,
And pushed the fellow underneath a bus.

Whatever people say about my son,
He does enjoy his little bit of fun.

An A-Z of the naughtiest children ever! From untidy Amanda and Bad Boy Benjamin to Naughty Dan, Greedy George and Sulky Susan. They're all inside, so open up and see if there's a poem in here about you…

£5.99   009940866X

THE LEAP

BY

JONATHAN STROUD

*He fell without a sound, and the waters of the mill pool closed over him.
I sprang to my feet with a cry and leaned out over the edge, scanning the
surface. No bubbles rose. There was one swirl of a wave, just one, and then
the surface was still again, as calm as ever.*

No one believes Charlie when she tells them what happened to Max at the
Mill Pool. The doctors and her mother think she is in shock; even her
sympathetic brother James cannot begin to understand.

So as she recovers in the hospital bed, Charlie vows to hunt for Max
alone. She knows that Max is out there somewhere. And to catch up with
him, she'll follow his trail wherever it goes – even beyond the limits of this
world. And she'll never give up, no matter what the cost.

ISBN 0099402858   £4.99

Also by Jonathan Stroud:
Buried Fire ISBN 0099402475   £3.99